RAVEN IN A DOVE HOUSE

"Your old dollhouse ain't nothing but a box of dust. Mama don't ever pay it no mind."

I nodded, too flustered to argue. Slade gently uncurled my clenched, sweaty fingers. "Here," he insisted, lifting the gun from Foley's hand and wrapping my fingers around the weapon's short barrel. "You're Fo's only cuz, Nell. This is family helping family, kind of like your aunt was talking about the other day. C'mon, Nell, be good to your own flesh and blood."

Foley was breathing heavily. His hands, now firmly wrapped around the can of night crawlers, were twitching.

I swallowed again, harder than before. The Raven .25 was heavy as a rock, and cold against the clammy skin of my palm. My whole body had gone stiff, and something had snatched my voice right out of my throat. I couldn't speak. But like a puppet's arm on a string, my hand lowered the gun into the pocket of my sundress.

RAVEN IN A DOVE HOUSE

Andrea Davis Pinkney

Houghton Mifflin Harcourt

Boston New York

ISBN: 978-0-15-201461-2 hardcover
ISBN: 978-0-544-23016-3 paperback

Manufactured in the United States
DOH 10 9 8 7 6 5 4 3 2
4500586849

To my editor Liz Van Doren—
thank you for helping me fly

RAVEN IN A
DOVE HOUSE

1

Daddy tells me that before my mama died, she used to sing me a song to help me fall asleep at night. I was just a baby, and as hard as I try to remember Mama's voice singing to me, I can't. But Uncle Bingham once told me Mama's voice was as sweet as an angel's. When I was old enough to learn to sing for myself, my great-aunt Ursa taught me the words to Mama's made-up lullaby. It goes like this:

> *Little brown bird, take your flight,*
> *Fly off and see the world.*
> *See kings and queens and castles bright,*
> *See hills of golden loam.*
> *And when you've seen all there is to see,*
> *Don't forget your way back home.*
> *Oh, little bird, fly home.*

Mama's song was playing in my head over and over again the morning Daddy dropped me off to spend another August at my great-aunt Ursa's house.

Aunt Ursa Grady is Daddy's aunt who raised him when his own parents brought him north from Georgia to live with her. Daddy never talks about his mother and father. Aunt Ursa is the one who told me about them. Aunt Ursa's baby sister, Ruthie, was Daddy's mother. She wasn't much older than me when my daddy was born. Aunt Ursa says Ruthie never married, and that she and my daddy's father were too young to care for a child. Daddy was a little baby when his parents brought him to live with Aunt Ursa. After Ruthie and my daddy's father left him, they were never heard from again. Aunt Ursa insisted that Daddy take the Grady name.

So Daddy grew up here in Modine, New York, a town people say is no bigger than a pig's knuckle. Daddy hardly visits Modine now or even stays in touch. And as far as I can tell, Aunt Ursa is angry at him for leaving town, going to law school, and not coming back to live. Whenever she talks about Daddy, she says, "I raised Wes like he was my own child, and what payback do I get? The boy has cut himself loose, ripped himself away like the skin on a cob of corn. He's forgot where he came from—thinks he's too good for all of us now. Him with his big-city attitude, wants nothing to do with regular people. A crying shame it is, too." If I'm within earshot, Aunt Ursa tries to lower her voice, but her words are just as powerful.

If my cousin Foley is listening, he comes to Daddy's defense: "Yo, the brother sprung free of this dried-up hole. Smartest move a man can make," he says.

Once, I told Daddy that Aunt Ursa thinks he's uppity, but he just shrugged. Later, I heard him tell Brenda, his girlfriend, that the people in Modine were "nothing but going-nowhere hicks."

Some people call Modine "New York State's Belly," because it's nestled right in the middle of the state. Others say Modine is New York's "Black Trap." It's a place where a small group of freed slaves from the South settled after the Civil War ended. But even with the town's low-down conditions—no industry, few jobs, no good land—the people have stayed and stayed and stayed. They've stayed for generations. Something keeps them in Modine—like they're trapped. "Still enslaved," Daddy says.

The story goes that Daddy and my mama visited Modine once a year at Christmas. On the Christmas after I was born, they brought me with them. I was still a tiny baby, three months old. Mama was real sick then. After she died from her bad heart, Daddy stayed away from Modine for good; he kept clear of Aunt Ursa and the house where she raised him. He even shut himself off from Uncle Bingham. Daddy lets me come to Modine in the summer, though. I've been spending Augusts at Aunt Ursa's since I was six. Now I'm twelve.

My school friends at St. Margaret's, back home, go to all kinds of places in the summer. Robin goes to drama camp in Vermont; Lauren flies off to someplace like Disneyland; and Danita takes a sailing trip in some water called the Keys, down in Florida. Tamilla, my best friend, spends her summers traveling through Europe with her parents. She goes to a different country each year. And every year, she invites me to come along. I always tell her no, though. I don't even have to think twice about it when she asks me, because I can't imagine a castle or big-steepled church that could top Aunt Ursa's cozy house. And even though I've never tried a French éclair or a German pastry, I'd bet a whole mess of money that they're not half as good as Aunt Ursa's cooking.

I miss Tamilla when I'm in Modine, though. She sends me picture postcards, and I send her letters. This year she's in Italy.

The last Sunday in July, Daddy dropped me off in Modine, like always. And, like always, I was welcomed with hugs and kisses and plenty of Modine's sweltering heat.

When Pip saw me, he danced in little circles at my feet. His bark was just as feisty as ever. "Hey, boy!" I scooped his furry brown body into both my arms, enjoying the coolness of his tongue licking me from my forehead to my collar bone.

Aunt Ursa was waiting for me on her porch. She came to the car and hugged both me and Pip at the same time. "This dog's been restless for you, Nell. He knows that as soon as the real heat sets in, his summertime playmate will be coming back," she said.

Aunt Ursa's arms were two fleshy pillows that wrapped me up good. She could've kept me folded in them forever, right there in her yard. Her hugs were the best feeling in the world. But after she'd given me one of her unforgettable squeezes, she couldn't resist holding me out away from her to get a good look. "Do they feed you down there in the city?" she asked, glancing from me to Daddy, who was still sitting behind the wheel of his new car, hiding behind dark sunglasses.

Aunt Ursa poked her head into Daddy's open window. "Wes, have they run out of food in New York? The child's a beanpole," she accused. Daddy's jaw went tight. "She gets plenty" was all he said. Brenda sat in the passenger's seat with her cheek pressed to the palm of her hand. "Plenty," she echoed.

Brenda's a trip. She and Daddy met last fall at a meeting for the Black Attorneys Coalition; they're both lawyers. Aunt Ursa tells me that ever since Daddy was old enough to go on dates, he's liked women whose brainpower matches his own. (Mama was a librarian, and she was as bright as they come, Aunt Ursa says.)

Everything about Brenda is smart—too smart sometimes. Maybe her brainpower is the same as Daddy's, but her mouth power is stronger than anybody's I know. Her words can be sharp as a razor sometimes. She calls me spoiled; I call her the spoiler. She's ruined things between Daddy and me. Before Brenda, I always sat in the front seat of Daddy's car, next to Daddy. Now I'm stuck in the back, listening to Brenda and Daddy get caught up in heavy discussions about why black people can't get something called "an economic stronghold."

Once, when Daddy and Brenda were deep into one of their brainy talks, I whispered that I'd like to stronghold Brenda around the neck. I didn't think Brenda heard me, but she did, and she told me to mind my own business. I wanted to tell her that *Daddy* is my business and that she was coming between us. But when I started to speak, Daddy raised his hand to shush me. He saw an argument brewing. Ever since then, Brenda and I hardly speak to each other.

Foley hadn't heard us drive up, but when he swung open the storm cellar doors and saw Daddy's car, he came right over. He was carrying his fishing rod and a mustard jar full of bobbins and hooks.

Foley is my all-time favorite cousin. Really, he is Daddy's first cousin, my first cousin once removed. Foley's fourteen, the only relative on Daddy's side of the family who is close to my own age.

"Yo, Nell!" Foley bumped his shoulder to mine. "I suppose I should welcome your bony butt back to Modine, but I got a *bone* to pick with you."

"What kind of bone?" I asked, nudging Foley back.

"A wishbone—I wish you'd pay me the five bucks you owe me from that bet we made last summer about who could spit farther." Even though Foley liked to bust my chops, it was all in fun.

I gave Foley a sideways glance and a smirk to go with it. "I don't play those spitting games anymore, Foley. It's gross to be doing stuff like that."

"That's right," Aunt Ursa said. "Can't you see Nell's growing into a fine young lady, almost a teen-ager?"

Foley nodded. "Yeah, yeah, she's growing, all right. But she's still as flagpole-skinny as ever. And she still got a score to settle with yours truly." Foley set his mustard jar down on the hood of Daddy's car and leaned his rod against the front fender. Daddy was busy blowing a stray eyelash from Brenda's eye. He didn't even notice that Foley had come into the yard.

"Hey," Foley said, giving me the once-over, "they

better stop feeding you so much; you're gonna grow taller than me. Soon we'll be calling you the skyscraper girl from the Big Apple."

Aunt Ursa shook her head and studied me a second time. "I suppose she *is* getting taller, but we'll have to put some meat on her," she said. And with that, she went into the house to get what I was sure was a tray of food.

When Daddy looked up and saw Foley, he finally got out of his car. The two of them shook hands. "Nice set of wheels," Foley said, gesturing to Daddy's hubcaps.

"Nice set of Nikes." Daddy bumped the toe of Foley's sneaker with his shoe. Foley leaned close to speak to Daddy. "That car ain't the only pretty thing you got by your side," he said in a low voice, shifting his eyes in Brenda's direction. Daddy gave a knowing nod.

Pip had jumped to the dirt. He was nosing Aunt Ursa's tomato plants when Aunt Ursa came back to the porch. "Pip, get your fuzzy behind away from there!" she hollered. And Pip had no sooner turned his attention to the roses growing at the base of Aunt Ursa's garden trellis—with Aunt Ursa scolding him away from that, too—when he started barking in his quick-yap way at a motor grumbling toward the house.

Aunt Ursa's brother, my great-uncle Bingham, was pulling onto the gravel driveway, alongside the woodpile, in his clunkety car—a brown station wagon named Buzzard. Rawling, Aunt Ursa's longtime friend, was seated next to Uncle Bingham. His full name was Mr. Dwight Rawling, but everybody just called him Rawling. He owned a small restaurant in town called Rawling's Fish Fry.

"That there is the fussiest tramp on Collier Street!" Uncle Bingham shouted at Pip.

"And the loudest," Rawling chimed.

Pip let loose another yap. Aunt Ursa waved to Uncle Bingham and Rawling from the porch, where she was setting up a tray table of cold drinks. "Look who's here," she said, nodding toward Daddy's car. "That's why *we're* here," said Uncle Bingham. "I was driving over to extend my welcomes to Nell and to Wes, and who do I see walking the mean streets of Modine but Rawling—carrying a sack of frozen porgies to stash in his restaurant freezer."

"They just got my order in over at Traub's, but Lou Traub's delivery truck has blown its gasket," Rawling explained. "And seeing as I don't got a car of my own, I figured I could work some of the kinks out of my bum leg by walking the quarter mile to make the pickup myself."

Rawling had a slight limp. Whenever he walked, his bum leg dragged a step behind him. He liked to call the leg "a bugaboo of diabetes." He also had a wandering eye that roamed like a marble in his eye socket. Aunt Ursa had once told me it was rude to stare, and she'd said it was doubly rude to stare at people who had such "afflictions." But sometimes I couldn't help it. That drifting eye was always looking up and off to the right. Still, Rawling had a way about him that made me feel safe, no matter where his eye —or leg—chose to stray.

Uncle Bingham said, "Me and Buzzard spotted Rawling right after he'd left Traub's parking lot."

Rawling shrugged. "I wasn't gonna turn down a lift on a scorcher of a day like this. And when Bingham told me he was swinging by your place, Ursa—and that Nell was back in town—there was no way me and my load of fish could refuse. A man would have to be a fool to pass up the chance to pay a quick visit to you, Ursa, and to you, Nell." Rawling nodded to each of us. "Shoot, you two are the prettiest Gradys in Modine, and pretty ladies help keep my blood pressure in check. So here I am. Came along for the ride."

"We can only stay a moment, though," said Uncle Bingham. "We got to get Rawling's fish back to his restaurant before it melts all over my chariot."

A little smile had come to Aunt Ursa's lips. Uncle Bingham and Rawling could do that to most folks.

Uncle Bingham kept on. "Still, fish or no fish, we had to come by to say a quick hello to our boy Wes."

"And to welcome you, Nell, Wes's fine little girl —who ain't so *little* no more, I see," Rawling said, peering over the top of his thick-rimmed glasses to get a clearer view of me. Daddy was leaning against his car door, next to Foley. "Good to see you, Bingham, Rawling" was all he said. He shrugged, keeping his arms folded tight across his chest.

I saw Rawling say something under his breath to Uncle Bingham. Then, to me, he said, "Come closer so we can observe you better, child."

I leaned my elbows onto Buzzard's window frame, next to where Rawling sat.

He extended his face to give me a friendly kiss on the cheek. "Look at this, Bingham," he said. "Our Nell's got herself bangs and pierced ears."

"And cheekbones just as high and as strong as her mama's were," Uncle Bingham added. I fingered the small gold hoop in my left earlobe.

"Come around to the driver's side and give your uncle some of that same brown sugar you just laid on Rawling," Uncle Bingham insisted.

Aunt Ursa had arranged several iced-tea glasses on her tray. "Have a drink before you head off," she called to Rawling and Uncle Bingham.

Uncle Bingham started Buzzard's rickety engine. "Can't," he said. "Remember, Rawling's got fish to freeze."

"Ursa, we'll have to take a rain check," Rawling said. "Or maybe you could bring some of that hospitality down to my shop. The prospect of a personal touch from you will give me something to look forward to." He threw Aunt Ursa a wink.

Then, quick and deliberate, Uncle Bingham stuck his arm straight out his car's open window to wave good-bye. He turned his eyes to the driveway and backed up the car. "I'll be by sometime soon, Ursa, for supper, a game of horseshoes, a tall glass of milk to throw down my gullet, and a fat slice of your delicious apple brown Betty. Make sure the milk's cold. Can't have brown Betty without cold milk."

I ran to the edge of the grass to wave good-bye to Uncle Bingham. Pip followed, barking all the way.

As Uncle Bingham revved Buzzard's motor, he said to me, "Oh yeah, I got something special for you, Nell—a homecoming present for you and that one part mutt, one part mangy, two parts alley dog." He extended his arm from the window again, this time tossing out a small rubber ball. Pip rolled in the grass where the ball had landed and yapped even more.

"And one part bark-is-worse-than-his-bite," Rawling added.

Uncle Bingham swerved his car onto the street and sent out a two-fingered salute. "Wish we saw more of you, Wes," he called out to Daddy.

Daddy was talking to Foley, letting Foley try on his sunglasses. He looked up and nodded. Uncle Bingham nodded back, and as he drove away, he hollered out to all of us, "Pray for a mess of rain, will you?

We haven't seen a shower in weeks. This drought isn't good for the soil—or the soul."

"What we need is a good soaker!" Rawling shouted, loud enough to be heard over Buzzard's cranky motor.

Pip barked until Uncle Bingham's station wagon rattled out of sight. Aunt Ursa said, "I don't know who's got a bigger mouth, that brother of mine, Rawling, or that fool dog." She hummed a little laugh. "Lord knows, I been putting up with—and feeding—all of them for more years than I care to count." Wiping her hands on her housecoat, she said, "Well, I suppose I'm a lucky woman. It's my cooking that reminds me that I'm alive, and that I've got something special to offer this world. And with Bingham, Rawling, and Pip, my cooking doesn't ever go to waste. They'll all eat whatever I put in front of them." Now Aunt Ursa was looking off toward Collier Street in the direction Uncle Bingham had gone.

Daddy came up behind me and gave my shoulders a little squeeze. "Nell, Brenda and I need to hit the road. You behave for Ursa, now," he said. "I'll call to see how you're doing."

Then Daddy walked over to the porch steps. He and Aunt Ursa exchanged some quiet words. I could hear only little bits of what they were saying. Aunt Ursa was talking about the first-ever County Commemoration, a picnic to remember the African Americans who first settled in Wolverne County. I heard Aunt Ursa tell Daddy, "You need to come home to pay a tribute, Wes."

Daddy said, "Don't start, Ursa." I saw him give her my spending money. And before Aunt Ursa could say anything else, Brenda honked the car horn. *"Wes,"* she called, "let's *go*. If we waste too much time here, we'll get caught up in traffic. You know how much I *hate* to inch along."

I shot Brenda a quick sneer. *"You know how much I hate to inch along"* came out an angry whisper under my breath. Daddy kissed me on the forehead, gripped Foley's palm in a good-bye handshake, and slid into the driver's seat.

Then, without a backward glance, he headed back to our high-rise apartment in New York City to spend the rest of his summer with Brenda. As I watched the gleam of his car's back fender get faint in the distance of Collier Street, Mama's lullaby flitted back to my thoughts:

Little brown bird, take your flight . . . and . . . don't forget your way back home.

2

On Tuesday, two days after I'd come to Aunt Ursa's, Slade, Foley's best friend, came by the house. "Yo, Slade's my ace—my boy! My A-number-one brother-man!" Foley liked to say. Foley wanted to be just like Slade—an ace, sleek and black. Ever since I can remember, Foley did everything Slade did—everything.

Simon Montgomery was Slade's real name, but he insisted on being spoken to "by the code." That meant calling him Slade and nothing else.

Slade was always cutting up, making me and Foley laugh. But even better than that, Slade's straight-toothed smile and big dark eyes had a way of drawing me in and keeping me locked up tight.

I was sitting on the porch step, watching Foley trim Aunt Ursa's hedges, when Slade walked up. The first thing I noticed was that since last summer Slade had grown from a measly sack of skin and bones to a solid stack of muscles. Maybe that was because, like Foley, he'd turned fourteen. He sure hadn't lost the bop to his step, or the swing to his shoulders, though. And he'd grown one of those goatees, with a smooth shadow of hair that extended up and around the sides of his mouth to meet a thin mustache.

Foley had grown a goatee, too. Well, he'd *tried* to grow one. But compared to Slade's, his looked more like a bunch of stray brush bristles that rested in a clump on his chin.

Slade eased his way to Aunt Ursa's porch, sliding his feet, just as slick as ever. "Now this—*this*—is a sight for sore eyes." He was looking straight at me, grinning with those teeth. Those teeth as even and pearly as piano keys. The teeth that accentuated his full, plum-colored lips. "Who is this beautiful princess, come to Modine?" he asked.

I giggled. "Slade, stop with yourself. It's me, Nell."

"Nell? Foley's cuz, Nell? The one who used to have spindly legs and toothpick arms?" Slade's eyes were still sweet. Still dark as night. Still deep with their own special soul.

"*You're* the one who was all spindly, not me," I said, hoping the giddiness that was racing up inside me wasn't showing all over my face.

Foley put down his hedge cutters to slap Slade a high five.

"Fo, man," Slade said, "you didn't tell me your cousin had grown so much. She makin' the flowers on that sundress of hers come into full bloom."

I crossed my legs and sat up straight. The skirt on my dress fanned over my knees. I pushed what little bit of chest I had against the dress's bodice. (That was another thing I liked so much about summers at Aunt Ursa's—no school uniforms.)

With a disbelieving frown, Foley looked from me to Slade, then back to me again. He shook his head. "I don't know what you're fussing about, Slade," he said. "Nell's a kid. A twelve-year-old baby, too young for you."

Slade hadn't taken his eyes away from mine. "Maybe so she's a baby," he said, "but she turnin' into a *babe*." Now Slade was luring me in with his stare, and I was gladly following along. "Nell's what I call a *butterscotch* babe—pretty-skinned, like I like my women." He spoke real smooth and slow, winking at me as he called me a *woman*.

I willed my shoulders back so that I could sit up even taller. While I smoothed down the hair around my temples, Aunt Ursa called from the house. "Foley, Nell, who's that I hear? We got someone visiting?" She wasted no time coming to the door.

As soon as Aunt Ursa saw Slade, she broke into a smile. "Simon Montgomery, how are *you*?" Aunt Ursa's voice rose high and whispery, like she was talking to a kitten.

Slade lifted off his baseball cap, which had matted down his hair and had left a halo of perspiration encircling his head. He said, "Mrs. G, did I ever tell you how good you look—how fine-as-wine you are—every time you wear that dress?"

Aunt Ursa sent Slade a playful, sideways glance. Her honey-colored skin blushed pinker than her trellis roses. "Simon Montgomery, you could charm the blue off a blue jay with your smooth talk." My head bounced in a nod, agreeing with Aunt Ursa.

Foley had gone back to hedge trimming, the snap of his clippers adding a sharp, metal rhythm to our conversation. Every now and then Foley would stop cutting to watch Slade, to study Slade's way of operating, to check out his knack for softening Aunt Ursa.

From his pocket, Slade fished out a bent-up index card. "Mrs. G, my moms sent me over here to see you. This is her recipe for macaroni and cheese. She wants you to read through it, tell her why the mac 'n' cheese she makes always comes out so runny. She's plannin' on whipping together a whole mess of the stuff for the County Commemoration." Aunt Ursa took the card from Slade and tucked it into the waistband of her skirt. "My moms can't cook for nothin', Mrs. G." Slade shook his head. "She tries, but the food always goes wrong."

Aunt Ursa came out from behind the door and sat down next to me on the porch step. I hardly ever saw her sitting down, taking a rest. When Foley glanced over, he stopped hedging, his open clipper blades hovering in the air. Aunt Ursa said to Slade, "Now don't be bad-talking your mama. She just needs a little help learning to swing her pots and pans, is all."

Slade rolled his soulful eyes. Aunt Ursa went on. "Simon, your mama's blessed with other talents. Goodness knows that woman can work a song. Ever since we were students at Modine Junior High, singing in the glee club, Rochelle could put flutter-wings on any tune. She and our friend Sis Midley could set the whole school to singing. With Sis's fingers riding the piano keys and Rochelle's voice rising up, everybody got in the mood for melody making. And me, well, I can keep a tune going good enough, but not like those two. The boys used to fawn all over Rochelle and Sis. In fact, they still do, every time the two of them bless us with their music down at church." Aunt Ursa closed her eyes for a moment, sinking into the thought. "Rochelle and Sis and I have been close all these years," she said.

Slade shook his head. "You ain't tellin' me nothin' new, Mrs. G," he said. "Miss Midley's always ringing our phone, talking to Mama. Then Mama hangs up from Sis and calls you. It's like you three got a special hot line going."

Aunt Ursa touched Slade's hand. "Me and your mother and Sis go back a long way," she said.

"Good thing Mama's phone cord goes a long way," Slade said, leaning against the aluminum siding on the house. Then he rested his sneaker on the hose spigot. Foley had finished trimming and was gathering the hedged-off shrubbery twigs in a plastic garbage bag. Sometimes he'd stop to listen to Aunt Ursa and Slade. Occasionally he'd glance over at me, looking to see if I was also taking in their chatter.

"I remember when your mama was carrying you, same time I was carrying Foley. Simon, you were an evil cuss of a baby. Colicky as all get out." Aunt Ursa smiled at the memory.

Foley tied up his bag of hedge trimmings and came over to stand by Slade. He leaned against the house, with the same twist of his shoulders Slade had. He peeled off his cap, real slow, and wiped the sweaty band of skin on his forehead, just like Slade had done.

Slade's hat was black with bold red letters that spelled out his name. Foley's hat was the same but opposite—red with black letters.

Slade slapped Foley another high five and said, "Blame my colicky-as-all-get-out on my mama's soggy mac 'n' cheese." We all laughed at that one. Even Aunt Ursa let out a chuckle. That's when Slade plucked a dandelion that was growing out from under the cinderblock foundation of the house. He held the flower up to Aunt Ursa. "With all due respect, my name's Slade, Mrs. G. It seems I got to remind you of that every time you and me get to talking. *Slade*, like it say on my hat. That's my name."

Aunt Ursa swung her eyes toward the sky. "You and Foley, and those hats. I think those things have grown onto your nappy, swollen heads."

"These hats is special, Mrs. G. Special 'cause I won them for me and my man Foley." Even though Slade was talking to Aunt Ursa, he was still looking at me, checking me out even more than before. He gave Foley a nudge. "Ain't that right, Fo?" he said. "I got us the hats."

Foley was curling down the sides of his cap's bill. "You ain't lying, ace. You the man—won the hats playing sitting duck at the Wolverne County Fair, last October."

Aunt Ursa was shaking her head, but I could tell by the tiny smirk dangling on her lips that she was delighting in Slade's way of singing his own praises.

Slade went on. "I won me and Foley's hats straight-up. Shot all seven plastic chicks with a slick-handled BB gun." Slade aimed his pointer finger at Foley. "Tell 'em how I smoked it, Fo—*bam, bam, bam!*"

Foley shot his fingers back at Slade. "*Smoked* it!"

Slade was on a roll. "Yo," he bragged, "smoked it *twice*. Hit all them sitting ducks two games in a row. Smoked 'em good! That's how I got the hats personalized—*monogrammed*, the way rich white folks got them shirts and briefcases and stuff with their name on it."

"A man's gotta have his name on his stuff," Foley said, nodding agreement.

Slade leaned in toward Aunt Ursa. "So you see, Mrs. G, I'm proud of the name Slade, proud enough to wear it on my nappy, swollen head. Simon's what my moms calls me, a potty-training name for the baby she still thinks I am."

With pursed lips, Aunt Ursa made a noise of disapproval. *"Humph."* She felt for the index card, which had become creased at her waist. "Simon's a name for doing right," she said. "When Rochelle had you, she wanted to give you a good, strong Bible name. On her birthing bed she vowed that the angels would ride on your shoulders, Simon."

Slade shrugged. "The only thing I got riding on my shoulders is that hokey-doke name—Simon. *Simple* Simon is what the kids used to tease on me at school. But yo, Mrs. G, I guess you can call me Simon if it does your heart good. But you—well, you and Mama—are the only ones I'll let get away with calling me Simon." Slade playfully bumped Foley's shoulder. "Mamas got all the advantages," he said.

Aunt Ursa said, "Now Foley, don't *you* go taking on some nickname. Your name's Earl Foley Grady— Foley after your daddy and Grady after me. You got that?"

"I know my name, Mama."

Slade's eyes had turned thoughtful. Glancing sideways toward Aunt Ursa, he asked, "You know *my* daddy's name, Mrs. G?"

Aunt Ursa shifted her weight on the porch step. "That's a question you oughta be asking your own mother, Simon."

"I s'pose." Slade twisted the toe of his sneaker into the dirt. Softly, he asked, "You know where my daddy's at?"

"No, child, I don't." Aunt Ursa shook her head.

"It don't matter no how. I was just asking." Slade shrugged.

Still holding the dandelion he'd picked for Aunt Ursa, he twirled its stem between his fingers, right up in Aunt Ursa's face. That's when I noticed the small gold ring that clung to Slade's pinkie. When Slade gestured, the ring twinkled with the sun's reflection. "Mrs. G, how about leaving me something sweet before I go? Something sweet and unforgettable, like you, Mrs. G."

Aunt Ursa flung her hand at Slade. He jumped back out of its way, tossing the dandelion aside, smiling sly and pretty the whole time. "Simon Montgomery, you've spent enough flattery for one day. Now put your flirty-boy eyes back in their sockets and get on home. I don't have anything sweet to eat today." Steadying her weight on the step rail, Aunt Ursa rose to her wide feet. "Bring yourself back here in a few weeks. I'll have a batch of macaroni and cheese for you to take back to your mama, a batch with all the kinks worked out. Meanwhile, tell her once I get my hands on her mac 'n' cheese recipe, folks at the Commemoration are gonna be lining up for seconds."

Slade slid his cap back on, pulling the brim down low over his eyebrows. Foley did his hat the same way. "You know I'll be back here long before a few weeks. I can't stay away from all of you that long," Slade said. "I'll tell my moms what you said when I go home, Mrs. G. I ain't going right home now, though. I'm gonna walk down to the train tracks behind Rawling's place. Gonna watch the trains pass by and wave to the high-toned people heading to New York City."

Slade clapped his palm on the bill of Foley's cap. "Can Fo come with me?"

Aunt Ursa was holding open the porch door, about to go into the house. "Only if you call Foley by his true name. And only if you wait for Nell to change her clothes, so she can go with you, too."

Right then I secretly thanked Aunt Ursa. Spending more time with Slade Montgomery was more than all right by me.

But Foley said, "Oh, *Mama.* Why she gotta go? This is a man thing."

"Listen, boy, take your cousin. Family is more important than any man thing," Aunt Ursa said sternly.

"Yeah, family," I said, smiling at the thought of being with Slade a little while longer.

Foley kicked the dirt. Slade rested his elbow on Foley's shoulder, while grinning at me. "C'mon, Fo, man; how you gonna leave a pretty young lady like this behind?" Slade tossed me a wink. I got all tingly inside. My eyes shot from Slade to Foley to Aunt Ursa, then back to Slade, who was spilling over with charm.

Aunt Ursa said, "Simon, you're a boy who knows how to do good."

"Thank you, Mrs. G," Slade said, all humble.

Before Aunt Ursa turned to go inside, she said, "Come to think of it, Simon, I got some marmalade cookies left from Sunday's church bake sale. I'll wrap them in a napkin for you."

"Thank you double," Slade said. And with that, Aunt Ursa left for the kitchen.

Foley sucked his teeth and threw me a smirk. "All right then, come on with us," he said.

Slade shot me another wink. He dug way down in his pants pocket and pulled out a roll of Life Savers. He curled back the shiny foil wrapper, held the roll up to my nose, and said, "Hey, Butterscotch, have a cherry on me."

3

The train tracks ran two blocks south of Collier Street, behind Rawling's Fish Fry. We shared the marmalade cookies as we walked, and finished them off before we even reached the junction of Collier and Hane. When we got far enough from Aunt Ursa's house, Slade and Foley turned their caps backwards so their names showed only from behind.

Foley playfully punched Slade's arm. "Slade, man, you one too-smooth-talking brother. Why you gotta melt my mama so Nell could come? How we gonna have any fun with her tagging along?"

Slade said, "Hey, Fo. Cool it, man. You got to learn the right way to treat your moms so she stay off your case. I can soften my moms into butter. She lets me do what I want, when I want, every time I slide her a little bit of flattery."

At first Foley and Slade were talking as if I wasn't even there. Then Slade took my hand and swung it playfully. "C'mon, Butterscotch, you know how to have a good time, don't you? You can hang, right?" I let my palm and fingers curl comfortably inside Slade's strong, dark hand. "Bet on it, Slade!" I gave his fingers a little squeeze. Foley shook his head. He dug his hands deep into his pockets.

We had just cut through the alley that separated Traub Supermarket and Vanguard Hardware, and were passing by the iron gates of Modine Cemetery. Foley and Slade were walking at a fast clip, their legs whisking together in the same easy stride. I had to take quick, choppy steps to keep up until Slade told Foley, "Grab Butterscotch's other hand. We gonna take her for a rise-ride."

Foley looked sideways at Slade. "What you mean? What *rise*-ride you talking 'bout?"

Slade explained. "While we walk, we gonna lift Nell so she be struttin' on air. On every fourth step we take, we gonna give Nell a rise-ride." Slade jogged ahead to show us how. "Like this," he said. "Walk, one-two-three—then lift; one-two-three—lift; one-two-three—lift . . ."

Foley watched with a doubtful frown. But I was giggling and ready to rise-ride. "C'mon, Foley, *do it*." I pushed my hand in Foley's direction. He shrugged.

"Dag, Slade, I ain't never even heard of no rise-ride. You and me are too old for that kind of baby mess. And why you gotta make me be acting sweet on my own cousin?"

" 'Cause *she* sweet, is why. And it's worth a lot of folding money to see a babe with a smile on her face."

Foley sucked his teeth. Slade went on, "Look at you, Fo—sulking. It ain't good for a black man to let his lip hang low to the ground, like you got yours dipping now. That's why white folks be dogging us, calling us liver lips. Pull in that lip, Fo. Help the race, brother."

Foley shrugged, like he was considering what Slade had to say.

"You gonna do the rise-ride with me and Nell or not?" Slade wanted to know.

Foley slid his hands from his pockets. "All right, Slade, man. I'll do it. But I'm only swinging her till we get to the train tracks."

Slade sent me a pretty-boy smirk. I smirked right back, just as pretty. "Fo, man, I got to teach you about treating women to some fun," he said.

Foley's forehead was wrinkled in disagreement. "I told you, Slade, she ain't no woman; she's just my cous—"

"Kill the excuses, bro; take up her hand."

I slid my palm into Foley's and set my legs to the same stride as Foley's and Slade's."

Slade called out the start of my rise-ride. "Ready, go!" He counted, "One-two-three—lift; one-two-three—lift..."

We didn't catch the rhythm right away. I stumbled

on the first count. On the second, Foley tried to lift me too soon. My right leg and hip thrust forward, leaving my left foot dragging in its wake.

But Slade kept counting, "One-two-three—lift! One-two-three—lift!"

By the fourth time around, we were onto the rise-ride. My feet swung up and out, just above the gravel path that led to the train tracks. And on the fourth beat, when Slade said, "Lift!" I let out a rousing *"Wooo-hoooh!"*

It wasn't long before Slade, and even Foley, were following my lead. The three of us counted together, punctuating each fourth step with a rowdy mix of *"Wooo-hooohs," "Yooo-yooos,"* and *"Hooo-hooo-oooohs."*

My head and belly enjoyed the dizzy thrill of it all. Me and Foley and Slade, on a rise-ride.

Foley's body loosened. And when I stole a quick glimpse at him, I caught him smiling.

As we walked on, Slade said, "Our fun is only starting."

Foley was panting lightly from our brisk step-and-swing. "Nell," he playfully warned, "you better watch this roughneck. He's *crazy*." Then to Slade he said, "What you mean, our fun is only starting? You not gonna show off 'cause we got a lady here, are you?"

The three of us were walking arm in arm now, slowing down our pace, approaching the train tracks.

Slade said, "Yo, Fo, it's like this. If what I got is worth showing off, you can't blame me for wanting to show it. Same way you can't blame a cock for flaunting his comb."

"Okay, man, but at least let me rest when we get to the tracks. We as good as carried Nell, and my legs is gonna give out on me."

"All right, Fo, but I can't promise that *I'm* gonna rest. You know how I get around fine women."

"Yeah, I know—cocky as a cockscomb," Foley said.

The Wolverne County water tower stood up ahead in the distance. Farther off, Sackett Appliance Company—the closed-down factory where my uncle Bingham had once worked—hovered on the horizon like a brick monster. The clouds above Sackett Appliance were as gray as the building's smokestacks. Along with Foley and Slade's talk, I listened to the faraway sky rumble a low, moody thunder. I remembered Uncle Bingham asking us to pray for rain. Maybe we'd have some soon.

The smell of frying porgies met us when we reached the train tracks. Rawling's Fish Fry sat just a few yards away, close enough for us to hear the music coming from Rawling's bar stereo. I sat between Foley and Slade at the edge of the tracks.

Slade pitched a gravel stone. It danced along the

crossties, then disappeared in the distance. "You ever wonder what the people on the train got going on, where they headed to, what they doing when they get there?" he asked.

Foley said, "All the trains passing through here are going straight to New York City. Them folks are traveling to where the action is at."

With my feet, I pushed the track gravel into a little stone mountain. "I been on lots of trains," I said. "It's just people sitting and reading newspapers and staring out the window, counting down each town as the train passes through."

"Yeah," Slade said, "but those people are moving on to someplace. To the Big Apple, where the big life is happening."

Foley shrugged. "You got that right, man. The only thing happening in Modine is unemployment."

"And folks sitting around talking about the jobs and stuff they can't get," Slade added. "But in the Apple, they got deals and dreams goin' on."

I crunched together my second gravel mound, realizing that even though I missed my friends, once I got to Modine I didn't really think a lot about New York City. To me, there wasn't much dazzle to New York. It was just the place where me and Daddy lived in a thirty-third-floor apartment on East Eighty-first Street, where they didn't allow any pets. It was Stewart, our building doorman, who greeted me with a single nod every afternoon when I came home from school. And it was wearing the same boring school uniform every day.

Slade swung his cap back around on his head so that the bill—and his name—faced front. "I bet my daddy's somewhere in the city," he said, almost as soft as a whisper.

Foley pitched a stone. It flung against a railroad tie, then smacked down into the gravel. He shrugged.

Our talk hung quiet for a moment. A trombone solo slid from Rawling's restaurant.

"The train'll be coming soon," Foley said. "I know how they run. Got their schedule in my head. The trains to New York—7:26 in the morning; 2:30 in the afternoon; 5:26 at night. The Washington, D.C., trains—every three hours on the seven: 6:07; 9:07; 12:07." Foley pitched another stone. "And sometimes it's just freight trains pulling through, coming along every other Friday, before the sun's up." He looked off down the tracks. "I been knowing these trains since I'm a little kid. The afternoon train to New York will be pushing through here in the next few minutes. Bet on it."

Slade lifted the bill of his cap and looked down the tracks, too. "Wish we was on that train."

"I don't wish that at all," I said, bouncing a pebble on my palm.

"Pretty girl, what you talking 'bout?" Slade threw

two stones at once. They bobbed and darted away. He said, "If we was on that train, we'd be headed for life away from Modine."

"I'd be headed back home," I said.

Slade scooted closer to me. He leaned in to speak.

"But hey, Butterscotch, you'd be on your way to the land of opportunity," he said.

"The land where you got a daddy with money to spend." Foley was backing up Slade.

"You mean a daddy with money to waste on his snitty girlfriend!" I let the pebbles on my palm drop to the dirt.

"Least you got a daddy," Slade said quietly.

I couldn't argue with that, though I tried. "You both have daddies—somewhere," I shot back. "What I don't have is a mother."

Foley had grown quiet, staring off at the power lines that towered along the tracks.

"But, babe, your daddy's got a lady," Slade said. "That's almost the same as having a mother."

"Hardly," I huffed.

Now we all sat silent, each drifting into our own private thoughts.

Then Slade gently curled his arm around my shoulder. "You sure are fine, Nell. *Real* fine." I could feel my skin getting warm. Slade's affection sent needle pricks to my armpits.

I turned toward Slade, sinking into the pleasure of

studying his face—the handsome spread of his nose, the strong high curve of his cheekbones, the quiet fire burning behind those black-as-night eyes.

Something inside me had begun to flutter. I never got attention like this at St. Margaret's—or anyplace else, for that matter. Even though we had assemblies with the boys at St. Peter's, there wasn't a single black boy at that school, and nobody who could even come close to Slade Montgomery.

Foley was absently pitching stones onto the train tracks. I heard him mutter something about Slade "always pushing to get him a tasty thing to nibble on..."

Now Slade was rubbing my shoulder, making easy circles on my bare skin with his hand. "More mouth-watering than candy. That's what you are, Nell."

I was holding my breath, but something was nudging at me. "You're fine yourself, Slade." My flirty words toppled right off my tongue. I blinked.

Foley shook his head. He had a crooked smirk on his face. "Slade, my ace, has turned into a hungry puppy—looks like Pip, barking up a skinny butter-scotch tree," he muttered.

Just then the train's iron hiss broke in. "Here it comes," Foley said. "The 2:30 to N.Y.C."

With his free arm, Slade pitched one last stone. When he heard the train, he stood up quickly. "Now it's time for more fun," he announced. "Bet I can walk across the tracks before it comes," he bragged. The train was nowhere in sight, but the grind of its wheels grew louder and closer.

I was on my feet, too, wondering if Slade was gonna take on his own dare. Foley said, "What I tell you, Nell? The man is crazy—stupid crazy when he's out to impress girls. And now he trying to make *you* his girl."

Slade hoisted himself onto his palms and started to handstand across the tracks. His sneakers dangled in the air as he found his balance over the skinny silver rails. I was starting to think Foley was right about Slade: crazy. "Slade, you don't have to prove anything. We believe you can make it across in time. Don't try it, Slade," I pleaded.

Now we could see the train's iron face. Its headlights and front grill sped toward us. Slade was wavering between the rails, moving slow on his hands. He was determined to keep going.

With the train just yards away, Foley hollered over the crushing squeal of its wheels. "Slade, man, stop it. Get down off your hands. Run out the way, brother. *Run!*"

But Slade wouldn't listen.

The train raced straight at him, and in a flash of silver, it blurred by me and Foley—*fweeeeesh!*

After it passed, Slade was gone.

Foley and I stood there pie-eyed. We watched the

train's silhouette grow small in the distance. The tracks lay empty. Mashed weeds and flattened wildflowers clung to the crossties.

I swallowed. Foley blinked a slow single blink. Everything grew quiet.

Then, from a grassy slope on the other side of the tracks, we heard coughing and cursing. "That train messed up my handstand!" It was Slade, coming toward us, brushing the dirt off his pants with his cap.

Foley ran to Slade. I was too rattled to move. All I could do was breathe relief.

Foley hooked his arm around Slade's shoulders. He hugged Slade to him. "Slade, man, don't be doin' stuff like that!" Foley was wincing and shaking his head.

My voice cracked when I spoke. "Slade, that wasn't funny. You scared us! Are you all right?"

"Hey, baby, I'm fine as wine."

Foley was helping Slade brush off the dirt.

I asked a second time, "You all right, Slade? You sure you're all right?"

Slade smiled pretty as ever. He said, "My hat got a little bruised, is all. And my cherry Life Savers gone and fell out my pocket."

4

Slade came to Aunt Ursa's again the following Saturday to help Foley count night crawlers. Since dawn, the two of them had been in the storm cellar, where Foley kept the fishing bait in a coffee can. Early morning was when most of the worms wriggled out from the ground, while the dirt was still wet with dew, before the sun came up.

"Night crawlers is a hooey of an excuse," Aunt Ursa said as she prepared to leave for church choir practice. "That boy is only after two things: my cooking and my niece. You watch yourself around Slade, Nell," she warned. "He's a good boy, but Foley's father used to look at me the same way I see Slade eyeballing you. Earl used to sweet-talk me like that, too, real whispery and smooth. Child, it's a heavenly temptation, I know."

I was sitting in the breakfast nook watching Aunt Ursa hurry around the kitchen and quickly slide bobby pins into a strand of hair that had fallen out of place. "Heavenly," I agreed.

The wail of a car horn rushed into the kitchen from outside, two short honks at first, then a long steady blare. "That's Sis," Aunt Ursa said. "She hates to be late for choir practice, and I can't blame her. Everybody looks to the church accompanist to be on time."

Aunt Ursa went to the screen door and waved out to let Sis know she was coming. As she adjusted the flame beneath a pot on the stove, she said, "Keep an eye on the food, Nell. Give the pots an occasional stir, and don't let the meat dry out."

The car horn sounded again. "Sis is nice enough to give me and Rochelle a ride," Aunt Ursa said, "but if she thinks we're gonna be even one minute late, she steps on the gas pedal with her whole foot—the toe, the heel, all of it—and I'm sitting in the backseat with my seat belt pinched tight as a girdle band, holding on for dear life. And Rochelle is calling out every stop sign and red light we pass."

Aunt Ursa tucked her hymnbook firmly under her arm. "But I gotta hand it to Sis," she said. "She's the only one of the three of us who's had the nerve to take up the wheel. And she gets us to choir practice—gets us there fast."

I followed Aunt Ursa to the door and watched her squeeze herself into Sis Midley's tiny yellow car. Sis says the only thing brighter than her car is the sun at noon. And nothing, she says, matches the fun of driving with its stick shift.

I fanned myself with both my hands, as Sis's car sped away. This was the hottest summer ever in Aunt Ursa's house. And today it was even hotter because Aunt Ursa was cooking her best to officially welcome me back for another summer. During the school year, Aunt Ursa works as the menu coordinator for the Modine school system. She maps out all the school cafeteria lunches and organizes volunteers to help with the breakfast program at Modine Creek Elementary School.

When summer comes, Aunt Ursa's free, same as the schoolteachers. The only menus she coordinates are for the meals she cooks me and Foley and Uncle Bingham, and anyone else who stops by to eat. Today there were collards and red beans with rice simmering on the back burners; a clover ham was roasting in the oven. Aunt Ursa's cooking made the air thicker than it already was. She always cooked Sunday supper on Saturday so that, when Sunday came, we could spend all the time we wanted to at church.

I could hear Foley and Slade's feet pounding on the cellar floor. "*Butterscotch!* You comin' to count?" Slade hollered from the landing, urgent, like he couldn't wait. "We need some pretty fingers to help us count these crawlers!" he called up to me in the kitchen.

"C'mon, Nell," Foley called out. "We need to finish this up before Mama gets back from church!"

Even though I was eager for more of Slade's heavenly temptation, I didn't want to let Aunt Ursa's cooking go unattended. And I especially didn't want to leave the honey bread she'd sliced for me at the nook. Slade and the honey bread were two heavenly temptations in the same house.

I checked the pots on the stove, then ate the bread down fast. "I'm *coming*! Hold your horses!"

When I got to the cellar, Slade and Foley were on the other side of the washing machine, leaning over their coffee can of worms. A single lightbulb dangled from a cord in the ceiling. It barely lit the room with its tired yellow glow. Under the light, Foley's face looked as pale as a winter moon. But Slade's dark skin appeared gray in the shadows; it was the color of ashes.

"Hey, Butterscotch, how you doin'?" Slade's eyes played under the dim bulb, like two ponds at midnight. Foley's eyes were a different story. They shifted with uncertainty. Foley was nervously tapping the tin coffee can. "We got a present for you, Butterscotch," Slade said. "Come here, by the washing machine." He motioned with his shoulder.

I was casually licking the honey from my fingers, certain Foley and Slade were gonna try to gross me out with some long dangly worm.

But when I went around by the washer, Slade wasn't holding a worm. He was holding a gun.

At first I thought it was fake—a play pistol or a water gun. But before I could say a word, Slade put a finger up to his lips. "Shh," he said, and held the gun out toward me, its barrel pointing down at the ground. "It's a Raven twenty-five, the best there is." I looked at Foley, who was anxiously yanking at the hairs on his chin, avoiding my gaze.

"Nell, you gonna do us a little favor," Slade said.

I felt my face, then the rest of me, go cold. It was as if somebody had suddenly pulled the stopper and was quickly draining my body of its warmth. I swallowed. "What kind of favor?"

"You see, Nell," Slade spoke real slow with a little smile on his lips, "I picked out this sweet little piece —the Raven—especially for my man, Foley. I got me one just like it. And what I got, Fo's got." Slade gave Foley a playful shove. "Ain't that right, Fo? You and me—brother-men."

Foley nodded silently.

Slade yanked the tail of his shirt up over his belt to reveal a gun tucked in the waist of his jeans. The gun's handle was small and black, just like the one he was holding in his hand.

"So what does *that* have to do with *me*?" My heart banged so hard against my chest that it shook my ribs.

"Foley tells me you got yourself a dollhouse," Slade said.

"Yeah, I got a dollhouse, but it's old. I don't play with it anymore. It's kid stuff. Aunt Ursa keeps it in my room upstairs, thinking that someday I'm gonna use it again." I spoke with hardly a breath between my sentences. Slade was nodding as I explained, as if he already knew about the old house.

"You *are* gonna use it again," he said, passing the gun to Foley.

Foley held the gun awkwardly. Slade said, "Tell her what you want, man." But Foley was slow to speak. Slade looked impatient. "Yo, Fo," he said, "don't turn into a sissy-butt baby on me. We been through this before. Every man who's going places has got a piece. And the Raven twenty-fives are our tickets out of Modine."

I was confused and scared and excited, all at the same time. "What ticket you talking about, Slade?" I asked.

That's when Foley broke in. "Nell, take the Raven and hide it in your old dollhouse for me. It'll only be for a little while. I'll come get it when I need it." Foley licked his lips. His voice had gone rattly. He wasn't talking right. It was as if he wasn't speaking his own words. And his eyes began to dart from me to the gun to the can of crawlers to Slade, then to the moist dirt floor of the cellar. "And don't tell Mama, either. This is between me and you and Slade," Foley demanded.

I was still confused. "Why don't you hide the...the thing in your own bedroom, Foley? Or down here in the cellar? Or outside someplace?" I asked.

Slade was quick to answer. "Foley and me thought through all them places already," he said. "But anybody with half some smarts knows you can't be hiding a Raven twenty-five outside where any fool can come along and get his hands on your piece." Slade stroked the hairs of his goatee. He said, "A Raven is prime merchandise—top-dollar steel."

Foley nodded as if he was agreeing with Slade. He said, "Hiding the Raven in my room is as good as handing it right over to Mama. She be looking through my drawers and pockets every chance she get."

Slade backed up Foley. "Most mothers be doing that kind of stuff. They can't help it. It's some kind of disease they got," he said, shaking his head as if what he was saying was a crying shame. "Once, I caught my old lady rummaging through my closet. When I asked her about it, she got the nerve to tell me she was gathering up my dirty clothes for laundry—like I'm gonna buy that sorry excuse."

Looking at me, Foley said, "Right, and speaking of doing laundry, you know how Mama always be down here in the cellar washing clothes, and stacking her canned cucumbers, and fussing in the meat freezer.

Ain't no way I can keep the Raven hidden safely down here."

Foley was right about that. The cellar was as important to Aunt Ursa as her kitchen. "Besides," Foley continued, "your old dollhouse ain't nothing but a box of dust. Mama don't ever pay it no mind."

I nodded, too flustered to argue. Slade gently uncurled my clenched, sweaty fingers. *"Here,"* he insisted, lifting the gun from Foley's hand and wrapping my fingers around the weapon's short barrel. "You're Fo's only cuz, Nell. This is family helping family, kind of like your aunt was talking about the other day. C'mon, Nell, be good to your own flesh and blood."

Foley was breathing heavily. His hands, now firmly wrapped around the can of night crawlers, were twitching.

I swallowed again, harder than before. The Raven .25 was heavy as a rock, and cold against the clammy skin of my palm. My whole body had gone stiff, and something had snatched my voice right out of my throat. I couldn't speak. But like a puppet's arm on a string, my hand lowered the gun into the pocket of my sundress. Foley shrugged and coughed anxiously into the damp cellar air.

Slade leaned into me. I could feel his warm breath coming at my neck. He pressed his thick, pillowy lips to my face, slowly kissing *my* lips. It was the first time any boy had ever kissed me. Softly, Slade said, "Butterscotch sure tastes sweet."

There was nothing left to say. With Slade's kiss lingering on my lips, I went straight to my bedroom. I creaked open the roof plank on my old dollhouse, blew on its hinges, and hid the gun in the attic.

My dollhouse had a special name. It was called Dove Haven. That's how it had been listed in the toy catalog: DOVE HAVEN—FOR GIRLS WHO WANT A HEARTH AND HOME. Daddy had bought me the Dove Haven house for my eighth birthday, and he'd had it shipped to Aunt Ursa's so I could enjoy it during my summers. Uncle Bingham had helped Aunt Ursa position the dollhouse on the cedar chest in the corner, and that's where it stayed. But each year when I came to visit, I played with the house a little bit less than the year before. And now that I was twelve, I'd outgrown it altogether. It had become a cobwebbed relic.

Aunt Ursa insisted on keeping the house, though. She called it my dove house, and said it reminded her of me and the happy "girl times" we used to spend together.

In summers past, Aunt Ursa had helped me keep the house in order. She'd made the lace curtains and the teeny bedspreads from scraps of fabric that were in her sewing kit. I'd spent hours pretending Dove

Haven was a real home, and once in a while Aunt Ursa played along with me.

The house was made with white clapboard, and real brick for the chimney. There were twelve rooms in all, each with its own miniature furniture. The living room had a little love seat, and an *escritoire*, which my friend Tamilla told me is French for writing desk. The master bedroom showed off a four-poster bed. Tiny dishes and flatware filled the dining room's breakfront, and a grandfather clock with a real chime graced the front hall. Aunt Ursa's homemade curtains hung at all the windows, and Uncle Bingham had helped Foley craft tiny hinged shutters that opened and closed. Dove Haven even came with a porcelain toilet for the bathroom.

The Dove family had a tiny figurine mother, father, and little boy and girl who I'd named Larson and Jill. Aunt Ursa kept the four of them seated in the dining room. Mr. Dove sat at the head of the table, his elbows bent to say grace. Mrs. Dove—she came with a frilly apron and plastic pumps—sat at the other end, ready to carve the make-believe pot roast in front of her. Jill and Larson sat opposite each other, smiling and happy to be part of such a perfect family. A family where there were two parents. A family where everybody got along. A family without a single unkind word between them. A family where nobody ever got sick, and nobody ever died.

Aunt Ursa waved him away with
t same minute, Pip lifted the lid off
et with his nose. When Aunt Ursa
om that, too, he started barking in
t a squirrel that was scurrying up
he end of the clothesline.

n with her hymn, softly humming
d. Then, like she'd snapped into
ed out, "Foley, Foley boy, where
e you *doing?*" The squirrel, now
the clothesline post, scampered
sa hollered toward the house.

k up Pip, who was busy gnawing my fingers, he groaned a

m the cellar, "I'm down here,
ting night crawlers."

Now, Foley's gun was sleeping in Jill and Larson's
home. I peered down into the house's attic before closing its door. My hands began to tremble while I lowered the Dove Haven's roof plank. As the hinges let
out a final squeak, I heard Aunt Ursa coming into the
kitchen.

"Good Lord!" she called out. "My rice-and-beans
have cooked away to crust. It's a miracle the whole
kitchen hasn't caught fire! Nell, where are you, child?"

I quickly made sure the roof plank on my dollhouse
was closed down tight. Wiping my palms on my dress,
I winced and cursed my forgetfulness. *The rice!*

I hurried to the kitchen, where Aunt Ursa was leaning over the steaming pot, adding water to the rice-
and-beans with one hand and adjusting the flame
beneath the collards with the other. "Here I am, Aunt
Ursa—I . . . I . . ."

"You left my cooking to suffer." She finished my
sentence and saved me from having to make up a lie
about why I'd let the food overcook. "All you had to
do was stir, Nell," Aunt Ursa scolded. "Stir and watch
the stove. Is that a hard task, I ask you?"

I shook my head. I couldn't look at Aunt Ursa.
"No" was all I said.

I was scared to speak, afraid Aunt Ursa would sniff
the secret of Foley's gun right out of me, right there
in the kitchen. But she was too busy trying to save
Sunday's supper, which was nearly ruined. "It's a good

thing Bingham's got his Masons reunion off in Denison and won't be coming over to eat this meal tomorrow. I'd never hear the end of how I'd served him a hard-to-swallow supper. He'll be by on Monday, though, and I won't have any decent leftovers for him." Without looking up from the stove, she motioned to the back door. "Take that basket of damp laundry off the porch to the clothesline and wait for me in the yard. We got wash to hang," she said, her expression busy with the details of Saturday chores. There was a brief angry silence between us.

"I'm sorry, Aunt Ursa," I managed.

Aunt Ursa huffed a little breath. "Okay, Nell," she said softly. "You're human like everybody else. You made a mistake, is all." She shook her head. "I'm sorry I hollered. I just wanted your homecoming meal to be special."

In the yard, while I helped Aunt Ursa hang laundry on the line, all I could think about was Foley's gun. Aunt Ursa was singing a verse from "I've Got a Robe," a hymn she'd taught me the summer before. She said it was a song that deserved to be sung "in full praise."

"I've got wings, you've got wings,
All of God's children got wings."

"Get on—shoo!"
her foot, and in tha
the clothespin bask
waved him away fr
his quick-yap way a
the post that held o
Aunt Ursa kept o
its tune as we worke
remembering, she cal
are you? And what a
huddled on the tip of
away when Aunt Ur
"Foley!"
I knelt down to pic
ing a clothespin. Lick
happy sound.
Foley yelled up fro
Mama, with Slade, cour

When
note,
tilted
her

5

On Monday a letter arrived from Daddy. Aunt Ursa left the rigid envelope on my dresser. Inside was an oblong folder. The folder was scrawled with Daddy's jagged handwriting.

> Nell, honey, I've decided to give you a special privilege. I'm letting you take the train home by yourself. I figured you'd like that.
>
> Here's your one-way ticket and a train schedule. Tuck them into a safe place. Brenda and I will meet you at Grand Central Station when you get back to the city.
>
> See you at the end of August.
>
> Here's a hug—O, and a kiss—X.
>
> Love,
>
> *Dad*

My insides slid into a pit of disappointment as I skimmed Daddy's note again: *special privilege ... train home by yourself…Brenda and I…* In past sum-mers—before Brenda—the five-hour ride from Modine to the city had been some of the best times I'd spent with Daddy. We'd count the silos along the way, and make up stories about the farms and factories we passed on the interstate. Daddy would ask me all kinds of questions about my summer. I'd elaborate on every sweet detail, while the hot breeze slapped my hand as it dangled from the car window.

When I read Daddy's note a third time, my thoughts churned an angry refrain: *Riding the train alone is no privilege. Seems like Brenda's getting all the privileges now.*

I sucked my teeth, slid the train ticket back into its envelope, and buried the package in my dresser drawer, under a heap of panties.

That evening after supper, while Aunt Ursa was wash-ing the dishes, Uncle Bingham and I played horseshoes in the yard. It was still light enough to see, though the fireflies had begun to flicker. As Uncle Bingham showed me how to pitch the shoes so that they would swing around the pole, he told me one of his stories. "The tale goes like this," he began. "You see, the horse, he got a new pair of shoes. But when the black-smith pounded them into the horse's hooves, the horse took one look and said, 'These is the *ugliest* shoes my horse eyes have ever seen.'

"So the horse sat down on his horse hind-quarters and unhitched those shoes. He told the blacksmith he wasn't wearing them. Then he pitched each shoe, one by one, at a skinny pole by the blacksmith's shack. Each shoe swung around the pole. Soon the blacksmith forgot the horse even needed shoes. The horse had made a game out of pitching his shoes at the pole. And folks have been playing horseshoes ever since."

Foley, who was looking on from the doorstep, rolled his eyes. He and I had heard this story a thousand times before. Pip tried to play with the untied laces on Foley's sneakers. But Foley wasn't having it, not on his new Nikes. With a flick of his foot, he said angrily, "Outta here, Pip! These Nikes are made with some serious leather. The last thing I need on them is dog slobber." Pip gave Foley a sneer and trotted over to where Uncle Bingham and I were playing.

I picked Pip up in my arms, while Uncle Bingham kept on with his story. "See, if that old blacksmith had given his horse some fine shoes like these here,"— Uncle Bingham tapped the toes of his favorite white loafers—"the horse would have been happy and we wouldn't have no horseshoe game today."

We had started pitching horseshoes before our meal, but no matter how many times Uncle Bingham had tried to show me how to pitch the shoes properly, my horseshoes never landed near the pole. I gripped one of the heavy U-shaped irons in my hand. "Like this?" I asked.

Uncle Bingham stood behind me, his arms curled around my shoulders, his hands guiding mine. "It's in the swing of your arm, Nell, from the shoulder, pendulum style. Work it real easy," he instructed. I swung my arm in a slow, steady thrust. Those horseshoes were heavy and hard to toss, and my shoulders ached after several tries.

"The idea is to land your horseshoe as close to the pole as possible. If you can get the shoe to wrap around the pole, that's a ringer, three points," Uncle Bingham explained. But still, I couldn't get my shoe anywhere near the pole. After a few tosses, I had to rub the cramp from my arm. Uncle Bingham said, "Did I ever tell you about Bingham Grady's horseshoe rules?"

I shook my head. "Nope."

"To my way of playing, everyone under the age of thirteen starts out with three points from the get-go."

"I'm *twelve*," I emphasized.

"Well then, you got three," Uncle Bingham said. "And young people get two points for trying, two points for smiling, and three more points for having fun. Those are Bingham Grady's rules."

"I'm having good fun." I was still rubbing my sore arm, but enjoying the shoe toss all the same.

Uncle Bingham said, "Let me see one of those Grady smiles so I *know* you're having a good time." I mocked a grin big enough to show off my gums.

"Well then, there you got it," Uncle Bingham said.

"Ten points for me," I bragged.

Uncle Bingham licked his fingers to wipe the powdered dirt off his shoes. "Ten points," he confirmed. "And you've beat the best horseshoe man this side of the Wolverne County water tower."

"The best in *all* of Wolverne?" I asked.

"Just you wait till the Commemoration, Nell. You'll see what I mean. Bingham Grady's gonna show everybody what real shoeing is. I got me a reputation to uphold—the *Grady* reputation."

While Uncle Bingham was busy talking up his horseshoeing, I noticed Aunt Ursa was struggling to get out to the porch from the house. The screen door was stuck. She was holding a tray and trying to push the door open with her elbow. "Can't you see my hands are full?" Aunt Ursa called to Foley. Every time that door gave her trouble, she got cranky. She'd been on Foley to fix it since the day I'd come to Modine. "This blasted thing sticks every time the air gets too humid," she'd say.

Foley just sat there, inspecting his sneakers, while Aunt Ursa struggled. "The jamb is swollen," he explained, not looking up from his feet.

"Well, get up and open it then," Aunt Ursa snapped.

I started for the door, but Foley said, "Yes, Mama." He was slow to rise. He licked his fingers, the same way Uncle Bingham had done, and wiped the leather of his Nikes. When he finally stood, he jiggled the door handle, then jerked it upward to force the door open.

"What has got into you, Foley? Where's your mind been lately?" Aunt Ursa's face was pinched with a frown. "You been preoccupied for days now. Help me with this tray, will you? And promise me you'll plane down that doorjamb, like I been asking you to."

"Yes, Mama, I promise," Foley said halfheartedly.

Uncle Bingham and I stood in the yard, watching the whole thing like it was a stage play. For two days, since that afternoon in the cellar with Slade, Foley had been keeping to himself, not saying much. And today he was looking real agitated. His mind was probably in the same place my mind had jumped to: Dove Haven and the Raven .25. He and I hadn't spoken to each other about it since that day in the cellar. An uneasy silence had begun to grow between us.

Aunt Ursa was getting impatient. "Foley, get me a tray table from the closet, so I can serve dessert."

"All right, Mama."

"And bring some clean forks from the dish drainer."

Foley was moving like a robot, like a boy without any thought to his steps. "Yes, Mama," he said again, more quiet this time, yanking open the porch door to the house. The door creaked shut behind him, causing its screen to shudder. Uncle Bingham motioned to me, and we went to the porch.

Aunt Ursa rested her tray on the porch step. When she leaned over, I could see her small gold cross dangling from a chain between her breasts. She never took off that cross. And now she was absently shining it up by rubbing it on the flowered neckline of her dress.

"And bring the plate of meat scraps I fixed up special for Pip!" she called into the house at Foley.

After a moment, he shot back, "I *heard* you, Mama!"

Aunt Ursa turned to me and Uncle Bingham. "Something's not right with that boy," she said.

"Ursa, he'd *turn* right if you let him be for a change."

I was pinching baked sugar crystals off the top of the brown Betty and sneaking my fingers into my mouth.

Aunt Ursa smoothed her dress. "Let him *be?* I can't let him be, Bingham. He's the only child I got. Ever since Wes went away." Aunt Ursa glanced at me. Now that she was talking about Daddy, I was listening hard. "And ever since Earl fled town, Foley's been my little man. If Foley ever left Modine, there'd be a mess of me in this house." Aunt Ursa shook her head. "Let him be—*humph*! I let *Wes* be. Now he never comes around. And Earl, well...this is not the time or place to be talking about *him*."

Uncle Bingham folded his arms. "Wes is a grown man, Ursa. He's got a life of his own. And Earl," he said with a sigh, "he's not ever coming back here, so you might as well face the fact, sister."

Aunt Ursa was watching the screen door for Foley, trying to ignore Uncle Bingham. But her tightened lips gave her away. She glanced over and caught me picking at her dessert. "Wait till Foley gets here with the forks," she scolded. Her eyes snapped from me to Uncle Bingham. "And don't you pay your uncle any mind," she said.

Aunt Ursa handed me a paper napkin. "You see what I'm saying about Foley, Bingham. The boy's been gone too long to be getting a tray table and some forks. I can't let that child out of my sight for a minute—*Foley*!" she called.

Pip lifted his scraggly eyebrows at the sound of Aunt Ursa calling. We all looked toward the house, listening for Foley to answer. But the only sound that rose up in the yard was the rustle of a new batch of wet laundry rippling in the warm evening breeze.

6

I knew two things about Foley's father, Earl. One was that he once loved Aunt Ursa. The other was that he drove the old Impala that slumped under the gnarly tree in Aunt Ursa's backyard. The tree had a permanent message carved into its trunk: URSA AND EARL 4-EVER.

"Earl's Impala"—that's what Aunt Ursa called the car—was green, the color of pea soup. Its tires sunk way down into the dirt, and they were barely supported by rusted hubcaps. The window on the passenger's side was missing. The cracked glass on the driver's side window was like a spider's web.

On Tuesday, the day after Uncle Bingham taught me to play horseshoes, me and Pip climbed into the car to pretend we were driving it. Pip sat next to me on the torn vinyl seat, gnawing at a broken windshield wiper he'd scrounged out of the car's half-open trunk. Aunt Ursa and Uncle Bingham were in the house peeling potatoes.

When Uncle Bingham came out onto the porch and

saw us playing in the car, he scolded us. "Come away from there. Ursa doesn't want anybody ever touching that car, do you hear?"

"We're just fooling around," I pleaded.

"Fool someplace else," Uncle Bingham said, and there was no mistaking that he meant it. He hardly ever got mad, so when he did, I didn't argue.

I creaked open the heavy car door. Pip followed me out onto the grass. After that, I stayed away from Earl's Impala.

Uncle Bingham relaxed himself onto the porch rocker, while Pip and I found a new game playing with the ball Uncle Bingham had bought.

Pip wasn't a running-and-fetching kind of dog. But he liked lifting the ball from my palm with his teeth and poking it around with his paws. And whenever the ball rolled into some dark hard-to-reach cranny, Pip could get it out.

"Roll the ball nice and slow. He'll follow," Uncle Bingham called from the porch. Pip whined when I took the ball from under his nose. When I tossed it toward the cellar doors, he trotted after it. "What'd I tell you? There he goes." Uncle Bingham laughed his belly laugh, a laugh that reminded me of Daddy's way of laughing. "Now, roll it with a little more grit, and that'll make him jump."

I flung the ball too hard. It bounced off Earl's Impala and flew down into the cellar. I watched Pip go after the ball, figuring he'd follow it and end up in the cellar, where Foley had spent the morning alone. But once the ball was out of sight, Pip was on to something else. He thrust his paw into the opening of a drainpipe. In no time at all, he'd pulled out one of Aunt Ursa's wooden clothespins and was keeping himself busy with that. Uncle Bingham did his belly laugh again. "That dog's always finding something. He's got a knack for digging things out of the strangest places. A scavenger, he is."

Then Uncle Bingham shrugged. "Well, Foley probably won't throw the ball back up. I think he's still mad at Pip for drooling on his sneakers." He shook his head. "That boy's got a mixed-up set of priorities. Sneakers aren't worth holding a grudge over. He's been brooding in that cellar since after breakfast. Guess you're gonna have to go get Pip's ball, Nell."

I shook my head, thinking it was best to leave Foley alone.

"Go ahead, now," Uncle Bingham said. "That cellar doesn't have any demons. Just fishing worms and your crotchety cousin." Pip sniffed the weeds near the cellar doors. He cocked his head and whined.

"Nell, you're just like your daddy was at your age, scared of that dark cellar."

I wasn't really scared of the cellar, though it *had* given me an eerie feeling ever since the day Slade handed over the Raven .25. But I agreed with Uncle

Bingham, hoping he'd let Pip's ball stay where it was. "Just like my father—a scaredy-cat," I said, not knowing Daddy had ever been afraid of the dark.

Uncle Bingham waved me toward him. "Finding that ball is for another day. You and Pip need to keep your uncle some company. Come sit on the porch."

Admitting the cellar made me afraid had worked. The ball could wait.

With Aunt Ursa's clothespin in his teeth, Pip followed me to the porch, where I sat on the floor next to Uncle Bingham's chair.

Uncle Bingham was eating apple slices with a pocketknife, cutting bite-sized wedges away from the apple's core and placing them, one at a time, on his tongue. A saltshaker balanced on his thigh, even as he rocked in his chair. He sprinkled each apple wedge before eating it.

"If Ursa caught me dousing my apple, she'd snatch this salt away from me faster than it runs from its shaker. She's always getting on me about my blood pressure. But salting an apple is the best way to bring out its flavor."

Uncle Bingham sliced off a new morsel. He trapped it between his thumb and the blade of the knife. With his free hand, he let the salt pour. "Want a taste?" He held the salted piece of fruit up to my face. "That's nasty," I said, pinching my lips together. "No thanks."

"Suit yourself." Uncle Bingham took back his

wedge and crunched on it with a slow chew of satisfaction.

Pip had settled into the dip created by my folded legs. Uncle Bingham offered him some apple, which he gladly took. He chomped on the apple, then went back to gnawing his clothespin.

Uncle Bingham kept on slicing, sprinkling, and eating. Between bites, he said, "Your daddy *loved* Pip's mama; Hallie was her name. She was a feisty mutt. From the day I brought Hallie home as a pup—your Daddy was a teenager at the time—he loved her good. Pip was one of five in Hallie's litter." Uncle Bingham was shaking his head, and smiling. "We gave the other four pups away, but Pip was too much like Hallie—a noisy pain in the neck. Nobody wanted Pip, and frankly, even though your daddy was already in college, he didn't want us to let him go," he explained. "And now that Hallie's gone to dog heaven, it's nice having Pip around."

"*You* gave Pip's mama to Daddy?"

"Hallie, and a whole mess of other gifts."

"What kind of gifts?" I wanted to know.

"Learning-him-about-life gifts."

"Like what?"

"I taught him how to pitch horseshoes, for one. And when he was sixteen, I taught him to drive my car. He was the one who named my old wagon Buzzard."

"Your car clattered back then?" I asked.

Uncle Bingham nodded. "At first your daddy wanted to name the car Rattle Bone. I didn't like the sound of that. But buzzards are members of the hawk family. They're slow-flying birds. I figured Buzzard was an appropriate name for my rig. Once Wes learned to drive, he took Buzzard all over Modine, with Hallie always going along for the ride."

"Daddy drives good," I said.

"He drove crooked till I taught him right," Uncle Bingham said with a chuckle. "Kids called him runt when he was a boy. He couldn't hardly see over the steering wheel."

I laughed. "Daddy was a shorty?"

"The Gradys aren't known for height. But Wes was smart as a whip. He had a good head on his shoulders. You see, I always believed in your daddy, always had big dreams for him. I knew he'd be the one to make it out of Modine, to the real life."

Pip had let the clothespin go and had fallen asleep. I stroked his crinkly brown fur while I listened to Uncle Bingham.

"I kicked your father out of Ursa's house, you know. The day he turned eighteen, I gave him the boot. Like *that*."

"What'd he do wrong?" I asked.

"He said he was gonna spend the rest of his life living in Modine. He said he was gonna get a job at

Sackett Appliance Company working on the assembly line putting vacuum cleaners together, just like I did for thirty years till they shut down the plant and put me and the rest of Modine out of work. *That's* what your daddy did wrong. He dreamed too small for his smarts."

Uncle Bingham finished his apple. He set the salt-shaker down on the porch next to his chair, tossed the apple core into the shrubs alongside the house, and snapped shut his pocketknife. For a moment he stared off toward Aunt Ursa's tomato plants, the vines that grew on a small patch of dirt next to Earl's Impala. Then he said, "That's when I told your daddy he was leaving Modine whether he liked it or not. I told him he was getting his patootie into a college. Morehouse College. He didn't know it at the time, but I had already written out the papers and sent in the application. Got him a scholarship." Uncle Bingham smiled at the memory. "You should have seen your daddy's face when I told him he was going away. You ever see a boy look happy and sad at the same time?"

"Uh-uh." I shook my head.

"Well, that's how your daddy looked on that day."

Pip shifted his position in my lap. His breathing grew heavier as he enjoyed his sleep.

"Foley sure likes Daddy. He thinks Daddy's lucky to have left Modine. He thinks Daddy's got it made," I said, stroking Pip's head. "Last year, when Aunt

Ursa sent us a Christmas card, Foley wrote on the bottom, 'Merry Christmas to the brother with juice. Wish I had it like you.' And he enclosed a little carved wood tree ornament that he'd made himself. It was a tiny model of Daddy's car."

Uncle Bingham nodded, as if he already knew about the card and the ornament. "Foley's always looked up to your father. And Foley's right. In some respects, Wes does got it made. You see, of all the Gradys, Wes was the one blessed with brains and talent. And on top of that, Ursa's always loved him like he was her own son, even though he was our baby sister Ruthie's child."

Uncle Bingham drew a handkerchief from his shirt pocket. He mopped the sheen off his forehead. "Foley, he's good with handiwork," he went on. "You know, fixing things, working with wood. But that isn't gonna get him the kind of success your daddy's got. See, Foley doesn't have the smarts that Wes had at his age—the kind of smarts that wins scholarships. And Ursa, she doesn't have the money or the inclination to send Foley away to college. Especially since it could mean that Foley would leave her and never come back."

Uncle Bingham rocked in silence for a moment, as if he was thinking. Then he said, "The sad truth of the matter is that Foley's got a lot of cards stacked against him—no real future and a mama who just about keeps him on a leash. *Pip's* got more freedom than Foley."

I nodded, agreeing with Uncle Bingham. Though I'd never thought of Foley in that way, what Uncle Bingham said made sense.

Uncle Bingham lowered his voice, as if he wanted only me to hear what he was going to say next.

"Now your aunt Ursa, she's a sweet woman, but at times she can be a piece of work. She's suffered plenty of losses in her life—too much for one person. First Earl left here, then Wes. For sixteen years, since I drove your daddy to the station and put him on the Greyhound bus going to Atlanta—to college—Ursa's been asking, 'How can a boy leave his own family?'

"But Ursa's got it all mixed up." Uncle Bingham sighed. "She thinks your daddy wants nothing to do with her and Foley."

Pip was starting to squirm again. He opened his eyes once, yawned at me, and went back to sleep.

"I know what Aunt Ursa thinks about Daddy," I said. "I've known it as long as I've known Aunt Ursa and Foley—and you." I shrugged. "Wish they were more like the Dove family," I said, quiet like a whisper.

"And with Earl running off the way he did, right after Foley was born, your aunt's been hurt one too many times. That's why she watches Foley like a hawk. Ursa's a good soul, but she's got a heartache that can turn her evil in a snap." After a moment of silence, Uncle Bingham said, "Some folks got worse bedevilments, I suppose."

"Aunt Ursa's heart must hurt real bad," I said, feeling my own heart ache at the thought of it.

Uncle Bingham said, "What I been trying to make Ursa understand all these years is that your daddy's staying away has mostly to do with Lacy."

I turned to Uncle Bingham, unfolding my legs, almost forgetting about Pip. "My mother? Tell me. Tell me about my mother." I gently set Pip onto the braided porch rug and stood up to lean on the arm of Uncle Bingham's chair.

"Pretty, your mother was. I remember the first time I met her. I knew Wes was serious in love."

"Tell me, Uncle Bingham. Please tell me. Daddy hardly talks about my mother at all. Even when I beg."

Uncle Bingham gently cupped his hand over mine. "I met your mama on the first Thanksgiving that Wes came home from college. He brought her with him. She was a student at Spelman, a women's college across the way from Morehouse. Lacy Nell Evans was her name. They gave you her middle name."

"Daddy at least told me that much," I said. "And he's told me that she sang to me when I was a baby."

"It's a right thing they gave you your mother's middle name. You look just like her, got those proud cheeks and chestnut-colored eyes. Pretty," he mused.

"But Uncle Bingham, my skin's light, not dark brown like hers. And she was a grown-up lady, with grown-up lady eyes and grown-up cheekbones and lips. The only things grown on me are my feet."

Uncle Bingham started to rock in the chair. Quietly, I spoke on. "And my mother had a bad heart. A squeezed heart that made her sick. Something Daddy says was *congenital,* whatever that means." I stroked Pip's belly. Softly, I said, "I hope Aunt Ursa's heart isn't squeezed like my mama's was."

Uncle Bingham shook his head. "Congenital means your mama was *born* with an ailing heart. She had a birth defect. It was something she couldn't help. What Ursa's got is different." Wiping his upper lip with the back of his hand, Uncle Bingham continued. "It was a shame, her dying so young. She didn't even live to see your first birthday." He spoke with a low, throaty sigh.

"Your daddy's been bittered by it ever since. He's done the exact opposite as Ursa. She holds on to love real tight, afraid it'll slide out of her fingers. But Wes, he's gone and pulled away from the people who love him the most—me and Ursa."

Uncle Bingham sat silent for a while, as if he was thinking hard on something. He slid a clean white handkerchief from his shirt pocket. "This heat's got me dripping fierce," he said, pulling the hanky taut at its corners and twirling it into a collar-shaped wrap.

Resting the hanky across the back of his neck, he said, "I wish we saw more of Wes. But I guess he's got to do what he's got to do."

The slow, creaky rocking of Uncle Bingham's chair made a back-and-forth rhythm against the porch floor. I played with the soft hairs on Uncle Bingham's forearm. Overhead, clouds floated past the sun to offer us pieces of shade.

"My mother's in heaven now," I said.

"Indeed."

"I look at her picture every night, before I go to bed."

Uncle Bingham said, "Keep looking at her picture, Nell. Soon enough you'll see your face in hers."

I sighed. "You think so?"

"I know so."

7

The best room in Aunt Ursa's house was the bedroom where I slept. It wasn't a fancy room, or a big room. But, oh, that room put me in a feel-good frame of mind. It had been Daddy's bedroom when he was growing up. That night when I pulled back my bedspread, there was a postcard from Tamilla that had been left on my pillow. On the front was a picture of a man rowing a funny-shaped boat. I flipped the card, and there was Tamilla's curly handwriting.

Dear Nell,

I can't stop scratching! The mosquitoes in Venice love me. I tried to catch one in a jar, so I could bring it home and show you how big they are, but when I stood up and leaned off the side of the gondola (that's the boat in the picture), I almost fell into the water. My mom snatched me back and saved me, while my dad tried to get it all with his video camera. Then my mother started to lecture me about how mosquitoes have a purpose, and like all living things, they should be allowed to roam free, even if they suck people's blood and make them miserable.

I really like Italy, but I wish my daddy would give his video camera a rest. I'll show you the videos when I get home. Just please make a big deal about how good they are. The camcorder is my daddy's favorite toy.

Write to me at the hotel address I gave you. I miss you.

Love,

Tamilla

I set Tamilla's postcard beside a picture of Daddy that rested on the night table next to my bed. The man on the postcard was smiling as big as the moon.

In the old brown photograph, Daddy wore a half smile. He was dressed in a graduation cap and gown, and held a diploma. His neck was skinny as a stick. Daddy didn't have a mustache back then, and his hair was shaved close to his head, almost bald. He looked handsome all the same, just younger than I ever knew him.

I'd placed the only picture I had of my mother next to the picture of Daddy. Mama wore a string of pearls and frosty lipstick. In the picture, she rested her strong chin on delicate, folded hands. At night before I went to sleep, I talked to my mother in the picture as if she were still alive. "Uncle Bingham taught me to play horseshoes," I told her. "And Aunt Ursa made some of her apple brown Betty." I thought to tell Mama about Foley's gun, but I didn't want to speak to her about evil things. "And so far the summer's going good, Mama," I said simply.

The wallpaper in my bedroom surrounded me with daisy buds. In one corner, the wallpaper was worn and turning brown, but those flowers were always ready to bloom. A tiny crack in the plaster on the ceiling over my bed never changed its shape. That night, like many nights, I lay in bed before I went to sleep, making up stories about that skinny black line. It resembled one of Foley's fishing worms. Then I turned it into a circus tightrope with an imaginary acrobat dancing along its curve. While watching the jagged crack, I thought about Daddy, and about Aunt Ursa, and about how each one was struggling with some kind of hurt.

I slid a pen and piece of paper from the night table drawer and wrote back to Tamilla.

> Dear Tamilla,
>
> I can't stop itching either! And I got plenty of reason to itch. I got a good itch and a bad itch. The good itch is a brother named Slade. Remember I told you about him, told you he was this scrawny kid, my cousin Foley's friend. Well, a year can make a big

difference, Tam, because now Slade is Pretty with a capital P. And Tam, remember when Danita told us that kissing a boy on the lips would give you some kind of spit-germ disease? Well that just can't be true, because (I hope you're not reading this while you're riding on one of those Italian boats. You'll fall off for sure!) Slade kissed me ON THE LIPS, and it felt like I was sinking into a cloud made of devil's food cake. I get a silly buzzy feeling every time I think about it. I even wrote a poem using the letters of Slade's name.

So fine
Lips touching mine
All beauty is yours
Do you know you're divine?
Everything changed when I tasted your kiss. . . .

My bad itch is like your mosquito bites, but it has to do with my daddy and Aunt Ursa. They just don't get along good. They have these mad feelings between them. Every time they have a little argument, or say hurtful things about each other, I get a sharp twitch inside that feels like when a bug bites you, and it itches and hurts and burns all at the same time. And then when you scratch it, it just gets worse.

Whenever I used to ask Daddy why he and Aunt Ursa ridicule each other, his jaw got tight and he started giving me short answers that didn't mean anything. He'd say, "Family's tough," or "It's complicated," or "Someday you'll understand."

He's been saying stuff like that for as long as I can remember. I'm still waiting for "someday" to get here, but it hasn't come yet.

Now when they have their little quarrels, I don't say much of anything because I don't want to scratch up any more bad feelings for myself or for them.

You're lucky, Tam. I wish I had a mother who could snatch me back from anything that might make me fall.

I miss you, too.

Love,

Nell

P.S. My daddy's favorite toy is his car.

I didn't dare write to Tamilla about Foley's gun. I was afraid her mother or father would get ahold of my letter. I folded the letter into a tiny triangle, licked the flap, and sealed the envelope up tight. I'd tell Tamilla the whole thing when I saw her in September, back at St. Margaret's.

I put the letter under my writing paper in my night table drawer. Then, leaning my head and shoulders off the side of the bed, I peered through the wrought-iron heat vent on the floor. That vent let me see clear through to downstairs. I watched the top of Aunt Ursa's head while she piddled in the kitchen, moving from the breakfast nook to the oven and back again. Pip joined me in looking. He poked at the vent as if Aunt Ursa's movements were a bug he could trap with his paw.

It wasn't long before Aunt Ursa came to tell me good night and to fuss over my room, which she often did once I'd gotten into bed. "Time for your beauty sleep," she said, plugging my night-light into the socket near Dove Haven. (I'd told Aunt Ursa a million times that I was too old for a night-light, but she insisted that "everybody needs a beacon in the darkness, no matter how old they are.")

Aunt Ursa sat on the corner of my bed. "Did you see the postcard I left for you?" she asked.

I nodded.

"Looked like it was from some far-off place," she observed.

I leaned back against my headboard. "My friend Tamilla is in Italy."

"Tamilla..." Aunt Ursa thought for a moment. Then a look of recognition filled her eyes. "Yes, I remember you speaking on that child—your best friend back in the city. Last year she was sending you picture cards with all kinds of castles and fancy churches on them."

"France," I said.

"And the summer before that—tell me if I'm mistaking—it was pictures of bulls," Aunt Ursa remembered.

I nodded. "Spain."

"Somebody who keeps close from so far away is a real true friend," she said. "Good friends are a blessing, Nell. You and I are fortunate to have them. I call that buddy-luck."

"Buddy-luck," I repeated. "That's something me and you got that's the same, Aunt Ursa."

Aunt Ursa shrugged in agreement. She rose from the bed. Then, like always, she started tidying. She picked up the shorts I'd draped over the footboard. She rearranged the barrettes, hair grease, brush, and comb on my dresser, and put Foley's old winter coat over the place on the rug where Pip was to sleep.

Pip sniffed at the coat, then took his comfort on its nubby fibers.

Every time Aunt Ursa went near my dollhouse, I held my breath. Tonight she was giving Dove Haven extra attention, gently wiping off its shingles and peering in its windows. I sat up in bed, my eyes fixed to the house's roof. Before I could speak, Aunt Ursa said, "This old dove house sure brought us some good times, you and me. You used to love to play make-believe with the little doll family that sits there in the dining room. And I loved watching you—learning, growing, just being a child." Aunt Ursa straightened one of the curtains.

"I was a little girl then," I said quietly, remembering how special Dove Haven had been to me. "But that house is no more than a box of dust now—it's not worth fussing over, Aunt Ursa, really." I was speaking in more of a plea than in regular chitchat. I prayed Aunt Ursa would come away from the house. But she was too deep in her reminiscing to notice the urgency in my voice. I was certain that at any moment Aunt Ursa was going to find Foley's gun; she had a way of turning up the best-kept secrets. With all her dusting and carrying on about the house, I knew it would be just a matter of time before the gun was staring up at Aunt Ursa from its hiding place.

My thoughts flipped back and forth like a just-caught fish. My lips went dry. I decided I had no choice but to tell Aunt Ursa about the Raven before she set eyes on the gun for herself. "Aunt Ursa," I breathed slowly. My armpits grew moist beneath my nightgown.

Aunt Ursa was eager to keep wiping the house clean. My anxious words came as an interruption. "What is it, Nell?" she asked, her face wrinkling into a little frown.

I shrugged. "It's . . . it's . . . Foley . . . and me," I said. From where Aunt Ursa stood, the curtains on the bedroom window framed her in white. Her dustrag hung from her hand. She looked at me straight, realizing I was making more than idle talk. "Who do you want to tell me about first? Foley or you?" she wanted to know.

I yanked on my bedsheet, pulling it closer, despite the heat. "Well...Foley." I hesitated. Aunt Ursa folded her arms. Her face tightened. I wished I'd never spoken. "It's just that the last few days Foley's been acting different than he used to," I said, lowering my eyes.

I knew that by not telling Aunt Ursa everything, it was the same thing as speaking a lie. A lie of omission—lying by keeping quiet—was what Aunt Ursa would have called it. I chewed on my lip, letting the omission lie sink its guilty feet into my gut.

Aunt Ursa returned to the bed's corner. Her face softened a bit as she gently took my shoulders in her hands. "Foley's just going through a moody spell, is all. Don't worry yourself about him, Nell. He's suffering from what I like to call the painful pangs of puberty."

I pulled my knees up close to my chin, asking myself if I should tell Aunt Ursa more. "Oh" was all I could manage.

"Don't worry, Nell. Foley'll come around," Aunt Ursa said, rising from the bed. She collected her dustrag, which had fallen to her lap. As she draped the rag over her shoulder, ready to keep cleaning, she said,

"You know, Nell, you got your own puberty pangs coming on. I can see them rising up every time Slade brings his sweet-talking self over here. I just hope all that stuff stirring up inside both you and Foley don't get the better of you kids."

I bit my lower lip as Aunt Ursa turned back to my dollhouse. "It's getting late," she said. "Someday soon, though, I'm gonna tidy this house from top to bottom." She moved in closer to Dove Haven. "A thorough cleaning will make this old house like new," she said. "Then we can admire it for the beauty it once had and the joy it used to bring us."

Before I could speak another word, Aunt Ursa lifted the house's roof plank and peered down in. With the cleaning rag still dangling from her shoulder and her hand resting on her hip, she said, "What in God's name is *this* doing in *here*?"

My breath snagged in my throat.

Then Aunt Ursa reached into the dollhouse and pulled out Pip's ball, the one Uncle Bingham had brought. She set it next to Pip on the floor, shaking her head, smiling a tiny smile. "That silly scoundrel probably dropped this in the house himself. I swear that dog gets into every place. He's just like Hallie was—just like her."

My body flashed hot then cold, then burned red again. Aunt Ursa turned out the overhead light. "Good night, Nell."

"Night," I said softly.

With Aunt Ursa back in the kitchen—I spied through the floor vent to make certain she'd gone back downstairs—I flung off the covers and stepped quietly to my dollhouse. Sure enough, Foley's gun was gone!

I couldn't turn on the overhead light; that would bring Aunt Ursa back to my room. But a small muted glow came from the light that shined up through the floor vent from the kitchen. The night-light helped, too. They would have to be enough.

I looked for Foley's gun, frantically, and as quietly as I could. Pip nuzzled his ball and watched me search each room of Dove Haven and every corner of my bedroom. I checked Mr. and Mrs. Dove's master suite. I felt underneath my bed. I slipped my hand into each roof crevice of the dollhouse, searching. On my hands and knees, I touched around the floorboards near the cedar chest where the dollhouse stood. I swept my foot behind my bedroom dresser. I even checked the thin, tight space between my bed and the wall.

The gun was nowhere.

Later that night, a wicked dream danced in my head. Foley's gun had grown wings and was flying madly around the house, banging into lamps and furniture. In the dream, Aunt Ursa didn't even notice the gun. But she clamped her hands over her ears when Uncle Bingham said, "You might as well face the facts, sister...face the facts." Then Aunt Ursa melted into a syrupy puddle that oozed into the kitchen floor tiles.

As the nightmare wore on, I was standing on the tree stump in the backyard, holding Pip under one arm and reaching up to catch the flying gun with my free hand. I couldn't grab it, though, not even when I jumped. Every now and then the gun would swoop real close to Pip's head, and he would bark at it playfully, as if it were a toy fluttering overhead for his entertainment.

The dream was a never-ending reel of moving pictures. Foley came running from the cellar to the yard to help me catch the out-of-control Raven. He was calling out, "This thing is too fast for me! I can't get a grip on it—can't get a grip." Then Foley started throwing his sneakers at the gun. He flung one, then the other, trying to knock the gun out of its crazy flight.

Suddenly, Slade appeared, looking cool and calm. He snapped his fingers once, and the Raven .25 flew down to him, resting itself comfortably in his back pocket.

When morning came, I awoke with a woodpecker-pain pounding in my head. I rolled onto my side and slowly opened my eyes. Pip's face was so close to mine that it startled my head back. I blinked twice, quickly. Then he blinked, looking as out of sorts as I was. It took me a moment to realize the bad dream was over and that what I now saw was for real.

Pip was standing on my pillow, holding Foley's gun in his tiny teeth.

The morning sun was coming in my window, making me squint. With Pip under one arm, I quickly put the gun back into its hiding place, this time pushing it deeper inside Dove Haven's attic and covering its heavy black metal with the lace bedspread Aunt Ursa had crocheted for Mr. and Mrs. Dove's fancy little four-poster bed.

Before I shut the roof plank of the house, I leaned into Pip's ear. "Pip, where'd you have the Raven?" I was whispering and scolding at the same time. "I was crazy looking for that thing. Now don't go nosing in my dollhouse anymore!" I swatted Pip on the nose. He retreated and whined, sinking his head into the crevice made by my bent arm.

Uncle Bingham must have heard Pip's whine. From the kitchen, he hollered up through the floor vent, "Nell, what are you and that silly mongrel doing up there? Come on downstairs. It's your daddy calling long-distance from the city."

I set Pip on his makeshift bed on the floor. "Stay put!" I gestured, pressing my palm into Pip's back to make my point. I dressed quickly, grabbed Pip, and headed for the steps.

Aunt Ursa's only telephone sat on a small table

near the staircase in the front hall. I leaned on the banister while I spoke, my finger tracing its curled wood. The waxy smell of lemon furniture polish clung to the inside of my nose. I had helped Aunt Ursa dust the front hall the day before.

"Hey, little lady, what's going on?" There was static on the line. Daddy's voice sounded faraway. "Did you get the train ticket I sent?" he asked.

I slowly twisted the phone cord around the fingers of my free hand. "I put the ticket in a safe place, like you told me to. But Daddy, I don't want to—"

Daddy wouldn't let me finish, as if he knew I was going to protest taking the train. "Foley take you fishing in Modine Creek?" he asked abruptly.

I shrugged. "No, but he showed me his bait." For a moment, I considered telling Daddy about Foley's gun, but the words wouldn't come. Besides, Aunt Ursa and Uncle Bingham were just a room away.

I was a tangle of feelings—angry at Daddy for sending that train ticket and choked with the fear of Foley's Raven .25.

"Does Foley still keep his night crawlers in a Roaster Brew can?" Daddy asked.

My fingers had grown numb from the tight phone cord squeezing at my knuckles. Somehow, though, I couldn't let the cord go. I was locked in its spiral, winding it tighter as I spoke. "Uh-huh, a coffee can,"

I answered. Then, "Daddy, I want to come home."

"Come *home*?"

"I miss you," I blurted.

Daddy chuckled in disbelief. "Since when did you ever *miss* me during one of your Modine summers?"

"Now," I said. Tears came to my eyes, blurring the phone.

I could almost hear Daddy thinking of what to say next. "Everybody gets a little homesick, Nell, even me."

"Homesick how?" I asked. "You're home already."

Daddy sighed quietly. "Sometimes when I'm putting my money down on the counter at Doughnut Express on Seventy-ninth Street, I get a mean hankering for one of Ursa's crullers. That's how I get homesick."

The phone cord was still putting a choke on my fingers. Daddy said, "Tell Ursa what's making you upset. She bakes a cobbler that can sweeten any sorrow."

I could hear Brenda calling Daddy. "Nell, honey, I gotta go," he said.

"Daddy, don't hang up—please, there's something else I want to tell you." Now my tears were making a slow roll to my cheeks. I'd wound the phone cord around my entire hand. My fingers were bent into a contorted knot.

"*Wes, we're going to be late.*" Brenda's voice shot up in the background.

"Sorry to have to rush you, honey. Can you tell me quickly?" Daddy asked.

I wiped my tears on my shirt and sucked in with a hard sniff. "Never mind."

8

In the kitchen, Aunt Ursa and Uncle Bingham sat at the breakfast nook with paper and pencil. Aunt Ursa's friends, Rochelle and Sis, were there, too.

Rochelle looked just like Slade. Her skin was darker than most—beautiful dark. She was small-boned, with full lips and square shoulders.

Sis was one of the littlest grown women I knew. She was no taller than I was, but plump in all the right places. Her complexion was somewhere between Rochelle's and Aunt Ursa's. When the three of them got together, they looked like a tribute to the flavors at Gleason's Ice Cream Parlor—Baker's Chocolate, Cinnamon Stick, and Pecan Crunch.

Uncle Bingham was speaking as I came in from the front hall. "Folks are going to be coming out like ants on their way to a sugar hill. You know how the people in Modine can't resist a good picnic. I suppose we'll be seeing everything from wheelchairs to strollers," he said. "The first annual County Commemoration is going to make a fine memory."

Aunt Ursa shook her head doubtfully. "It might take a few Commemorations for people to catch on. We may not attract as many people as we'd like, this being the first one."

Uncle Bingham was leaning back in his chair. "Ursa, when the word spreads that there's gonna be plenty of food and a whole mess of fun, people will come to get it all."

"Everybody likes to party," Sis said.

"And the folks in this county love to eat—especially when you're doing some of the cooking, Ursa," said Rochelle.

Aunt Ursa pointed to the paper where Uncle Bingham was writing. "Says here we got to fill this whole thing out in full," she said.

"Why do we have to sign a paper to sell a few cakes?" Sis wanted to know.

Rochelle rested her hand on her hip. She shook her head, as if she was being wronged somehow.

Uncle Bingham started writing again. "Listen, you three are the ones who came up with the idea to raise money for a County Commemoration marker to be set out in front of Town Hall. A permanent remembrance of the men and women who founded this county is a fine-hearted notion." Now Uncle Bingham was gesturing with his pencil toward Aunt Ursa, Rochelle, and Sis. "If charging for your cakes and pies is the way you want to scrounge up the money, then you've got to follow rules. You need this permit. And so do all the other ladies you've got lined up to sell their meats and slaws and beans and rices."

I leaned in the kitchen doorway, my arms folded tight. "What'd your daddy have to say?" Uncle Bingham asked.

"He said for Aunt Ursa to make me some cobbler." I had wiped my tears clean, but a heavy lump still hung in my throat.

Aunt Ursa was watching Uncle Bingham fill out the permit. "That all he say? Is he coming to the Commemoration?" she asked.

"We didn't talk about that," I said.

Uncle Bingham stopped writing and placed his hand on Aunt Ursa's forearm as if he sensed she was getting more riled up. Aunt Ursa shot him a sideways frown.

"Bingham, I'm just *asking*," she said.

"Ursa, it's not good to ask a question you want answered with a yes when you know full well that the answer is a *no*."

A blue black housefly was floating at my ear. I shooed it away, but it was back to pestering me in no time.

"Maybe Wes has changed his mind," Aunt Ursa said. "If he *is* coming to the Commemoration, I need to know, so I can bake him some maple cake."

Rochelle nodded agreement. "Wes used to down your cake like it was the last cake he'd ever eat in his lifetime," she said.

"Used to chew it real slow—like it was cud," Sis added with a little laugh.

Watching Aunt Ursa with her friends eased some of my upset.

Aunt Ursa looked off out the window, as if she was taking in a memory. "Yeah, Wes has always loved my maple cake," she said softly.

Uncle Bingham said, "Ursa, you're daydreaming again, and now you got your twin sisters singing back-up. Wes hasn't eaten your maple cake in years, but here's the next best thing—Wes's girl asking for some cobbler."

Aunt Ursa looked from me to Rochelle to Sis to Uncle Bingham. Her lips tightened, causing her chin to push up into a wrinkle. "I'm *not* daydreaming, Bingham. I'm a woman with a strong faith—faith in the good intentions of people. There's nothing wrong with *that*."

The housefly finally buzzed away from me. Now he was bobbing near the spinning window fan. "You got any cobbler made, Aunt Ursa?" I asked. Aunt Ursa rose from her chair, her lips still pursed. She went to the refrigerator to pull out a foil-covered tin. "Wash your hands, child. I'll slice you some raisin pie. I don't have any cobbler today." Uncle Bingham shook his head and went back to filling out the permit. Sis and Rochelle were mumbling something about women *needing* to back up each other.

While I washed my hands, I stared out the kitchen window. I ran my fingers under a stream of cool water, then picked up the soap in the dish on the sill. Sliding my palms around that block of Ivory reminded me of a day last summer when Foley showed me how he carved animals out of soap. That long-ago day was a Saturday.

"Hell-hot" is what Uncle Bingham had called it, before he and Aunt Ursa left in his station wagon for the Traub Supermarket. Me and Foley were sitting in the yard, under the tree that had URSA AND EARL 4-EVER etched into its bark. Pip was there, too, sleeping on his back, his short legs dangling, his thirsty tongue hanging out the side of his mouth. Foley gripped a new bar of Ivory soap firmly in one hand. He held Aunt Ursa's paring knife in the other.

"Wanna see me turn this soap into Pip?" he asked.

"How you gonna do *that?*" I wanted to know.

"Easy. Watch this."

Foley sliced into a corner of the soap, rounding its pointy edge with the knife. "First you got to get rid of the square shape. You got to give the soap some kind of life." Foley carved away all the hard edges, turning the white block into an egg-shaped oval.

He studied Pip for a moment. Then he carefully whittled away at the shapeless hunk until two nubs began to resemble dog paws. By sliding the knife's blade around the broad part of the oval, Foley fashioned Pip's belly. He curled the blade in, then drew it abruptly outward to make a notch that helped shape a tail. While he carved, Foley's eyes leaped along the contour of his soap sculpture, admiring his design. Pride brightened his face.

With careful, even strokes, Foley worked at his miniature dog until, more and more, it resembled Pip—from his tail to his tongue—sleeping there in front of us.

I watched every move of Foley's nimble brown fingers, sculpting the soap like it truly was fine ivory. "Where'd you learn to do that, Foley?" I asked.

"Taught myself," Foley said, concentrating on his handiwork.

I blinked. "It's *good*, Foley," I said.

To finish his carving, Foley etched out a dog nose and muzzle. With the knife's point, he detailed tiny eyes, then nostrils. I said, "Foley, you could be a real live artist."

Foley blew on his sculpture to get rid of the stray shavings stuck to its surface. "My real wish is to be a carpenter," he said. "I wanna turn people's old slabs of wood into table legs and footstools and cabinets and clocks. Soon as I'm grown, that's what I'm'a do. Be a carpenter," Foley said.

"You'd make a fine carpenter, Foley. And when you get to be one, how about you carving me a little bird to decorate the chimney of my dollhouse?"

"If there ever gets to be any summer carpentry jobs in Modine, you got yourself a deal." Foley had promised me that on that far-gone summer day. But he hadn't carved me that Ivory soap bird—he'd never found a carpentry job. Standing there at the sink, I wondered if Foley even remembered his promise from a year ago. I knew he'd kept his dream of becoming a carpenter. That was something he wouldn't let anyone forget.

Like a pin piercing a bubble, Aunt Ursa's voice broke into my memory of Foley's soap carving. "Nell—Nell, child, stop letting the water run on like that. And stop playing with the soap. Dry your hands and come eat your pie."

"You'd best come get it quick, Nell," Uncle Bingham said, "before *I* eat the pie. And don't forget your milk." Uncle Bingham waved his finger at the pie plate. "It's like I always say. Pies and such don't taste right without milk poured down your gullet."

I turned off the running water, wiped my hands on the dish towel that was tucked into the cabinet handle, and let the memory of Foley's soap sculpture linger in my thoughts.

After that day under the tree, Foley had carved a whole animal collection—a monkey, a cat, an alligator, two crayfish, and a jackrabbit—all out of soap. He lined up the figures along the windowsill in the kitchen, like they were marching in a parade. He had let me keep the one he had made of Pip. I floated that tiny dog statuette—on his back, the same way he slept under the tree—on top of my bathwater every night for almost two weeks. But eventually the water and the bath steam had melted Pip down to what he had started out as—a blob of soap.

Now, in Aunt Ursa's kitchen, the windowsill stood mostly bare, except for the ceramic soap dish, a wet Brillo pad, and a bottle of Jergens hand lotion.

I stayed at the sink for a minute, fiddling with the dish towel. I wondered what had ever happened to Foley's soap animals. And I wondered if Aunt Ursa ever found out that Foley was using her paring knife to make them.

9

The next morning, Foley brought a deck of cards out to the yard. We sat at the picnic table, near the tree that was engraved with Aunt Ursa's and Earl's names. Foley wore a heavy expression, like he was weighing his thoughts. He and I hadn't spoken much in the last week or so and I was glad to see that he was up for cards. He cut the deck for a game of war.

"Foley, remember last summer when I beat you at war three times in a row?"

"Yeah," Foley said absently, as he threw down a three of hearts.

I put down a six of diamonds. My card being higher, I took Foley's three into my hand. "We bet a dollar on who would win each game," I reminded him.

"Uh-huh" was all Foley said. His mind was still somewhere else, but at least the strained silence that had hung between us was giving way.

I tried to break through to Foley by elbowing him

"And Mama's *face*," Foley said. "The way she was scowling at you when you asked about Snake. She frowned so hard her eyebrows looked like a hairy letter *V*." Foley got control of himself. He put his cap back on. His laughter slowly died down. "Yeah," he said, "Mama's a trip."

I was enjoying the giggly tickle inside my belly. But the laughing turned serious when Foley said, "This summer, if we find another Snake, you could keep him in your old dollhouse. Mama won't look there."

I slid Foley a cautious glance. "I got enough in my Dove Haven as it is," I said.

"You still got my piece?" he asked.

I nodded, then lowered my eyes. The chilly blood-rush that had come to me when I was in the cellar was clutching at my insides again. "Where'd Slade get that thing anyway?" I wanted to know.

"In the parking lot, behind Rawling's Fish Fry," Foley said plainly. "Slade, he knows a brother with a car trunk full of pieces. Slade got our Ravens from him."

Even with that icy feeling rising up from my belly, my hands had grown sweaty.

"What are you and Slade gonna do with... with the Raven twenty-fives?" I asked.

Foley looked serious. "We gonna leave here, Nell, kiss Modine a sweet good-bye. The Ravens are our tickets out."

"What kind of tickets?"

"*Fast* tickets."

"To where?"

"To the city—New York. Slade and me, we gonna be big men, like your daddy. We gonna live, baby. *Live.*"

"Live?"

"That's right. Slade says we can make some easy money. All we gotta do is sell our Ravens to a brother Slade's cousin works for. Slade says the brother will pay top dollar for the Ravens and hook us up with some kind of jobs. I might even be able to get me a carpentry gig."

Foley messed with his cards on the table. "All's I want is to work with wood and my hands," he said softly. "All's I want is a chance to do my thing. Slade says they got plenty of jobs in the Big Apple, and that the Ravens is the quick boost we need to get hooked up—to make some connections." Foley kicked the tree roots growing up through the dirt. He punched the air in front of him. "With a job in my back pocket, I'm home free. A city man, like your pops," he said.

I licked my lips, which had grown dry in the afternoon's heat. "Foley," I said slowly, "the Ravens aren't the way. Those guns are bad news—trouble."

Foley shrugged. His eyes avoided mine. He was frowning a serious frown, thinking hard on something.

I told Foley about my nightmare, and how Pip had

gotten to the Raven, and how Aunt Ursa was snooping around Dove Haven. "That gun's not gonna stay a secret for long, Foley," I said. "I'm scared of what that thing can do. It's evil, Foley."

Foley gave a slow nod, like he was agreeing with me. I leaned in toward him. "You oughta give the Raven back to Slade, tell him you're gonna get your own ticket out of Modine," I said.

Foley picked up the cards on the table and shuffled them over and over. After a moment, he said, "Maybe the Ravens *ain't* such a good idea, but I don't got no other way to make a break from Modine. Besides, Slade's like my own brother. He ain't never steered me wrong yet. Slade's smart. He knows what it takes to make the move—to get something more than we got here."

Foley kept shuffling the cards. While he spoke, his shuffling grew faster and more deliberate. "Slade and me, we been tight since day one. We're as close as two fingers. Ever since we were little kids, Slade's been looking out for me, Nell. Like in grade school, me and Slade were always the skinniest, shortest kids. And on top of that, I was shy, always picked last for speedball, and slow to raise my hand in class. When Slade and me were together, kids called us Shorty and Slim. And Slade, he had to deal with his name being Simon— *Simple* Simon, like they used to tease."

Even though I'd known Slade when he was skinny

and small, it was hard to think of anybody making fun of him now that he was so fine.

Foley kept on remembering. "You see, Nell," he said, "some kids were real mean back then. But Slade, he could outthink them all, especially when it came to his name. He always had a quick comeback, but he never hurt nobody when he was defending himself.

"There was this one kid, Booker Lee, who wouldn't let up on the Simple Simon thing. Slade let it go for weeks. He turned the other cheek. He tried to ignore that wise guy. Then one day Booker wouldn't shut up about it. 'Simple Simon. Simple Simon.' He chanted it over and over, like a song. I could see how it was getting to Slade. And boy, if it had been me, I would have tried to pound Booker, even though he was bigger than I was.

"But one day Slade turned to the guy and said, 'If I'm Simple Simon, then I'm the one who met the pie man going to the fair. So that means I'm the brother who got all the sweets to eat—the best pies in town, all to myself.'

"Well, Booker couldn't say nothing to that. So he turned his attention to picking on me, and started calling me stuff like the Modine mutant, on account of my size. I couldn't think on my feet like Slade's always been able to do, so I would just try to shrug it off.

"After a while of this, Slade noticed what was going on, and every time Booker got up in my face, Slade would say, real seriously, 'You better not mess with Foley. He may be small, but he knows karate. I've seen him use it plenty of times. I feel sorry for all those kids he's chopped up with his bare hands.' "

I couldn't help but laugh when Foley was telling me this story. It wasn't hard to picture Slade stretching the truth to help Foley. But the funny thing was that Foley would never harm a flea. Even if he knew karate, the last thing he'd use it for would be to hurt somebody.

But then Foley started telling more about Booker Lee, and an angry expression tugged at his face. "No-pops—that's the name Booker used to call both Slade and me," he said. " 'Here come the no-pops—two losers who ain't got no daddy.' Man, Booker just thought that was so funny. He loved to holler it out on the playground—'No-pops, no-pops, no-pops!'

"Well, Slade didn't have a good comeback for that one." Foley's jaw got tight. "Don't think he didn't try, though."

"What'd Slade do?" I asked.

Foley got a faraway look in his eyes. "He just pulled me up in a funny headlock, like we were glued together somehow, then he said, 'Yo, *Foley's* my pops, and I'm his.'

"I remember thinking that didn't really make no sense, but I looked right in Booker's face and said, 'Yeah, this here's Slade, my old man.' "

Right then, I remembered what Aunt Ursa had said about good friends. Foley had been blessed with buddy-luck, too.

The sun sat high overhead now, sending off the day's harshest heat. Foley abandoned his cards altogether, letting them sit there in front of him. He leaned forward on his picnic bench, propped his elbows on the table, and rested his forehead on clenched fists. Then he started in with another story about Slade.

"In sixth grade Slade and I went out for the Modine Marlins basketball team," he began. Foley was sinking deep into remembering. It was as if he wasn't speaking to anybody in particular. He was just reminiscing for the sake of memory. "I knew I didn't have a chance in hell of making that team," he continued, "but Slade encouraged me to try out with him. I couldn't pass or shoot for nothing, and everybody trying out on that court knew it, too. But Slade, he could weave and dodge and fake and dribble like nobody else. He had all the right moves. And because he was small, he could work his way down the court, fast, and sly as a fox. Not like them big tall guys who were mostly legs.

"During tryouts lots of girls hung out at the court, and Slade was starting to win them over. Even Booker Lee was there, and when he watched Slade play hoop, he had respect written all over his face." Foley started to bend the bill on his cap, shading his eyes even more from the sun.

I shrugged. "Did Slade make the team?" I asked.

"One of the first ones picked," Foley said.

"And you?"

"One of the first to be cut."

"That's lousy, Foley," I said.

Foley snorted a little laugh. "When the news came down about who'd made the team and who'd been booted, Slade refused to join the Marlins unless they included me, too," he explained. "When the coach tried to tell Slade that I didn't have what it takes to play ball, Slade just shook his head and said, 'I don't play unless Foley plays. That's just the way it is.'

"Slade said it real loud, in front of all those girls and in front of Booker. When the coach refused to let me on the team, Slade took one look at me and said, 'C'mon, Fo, you and me, we'll be our own team.'"

Now Foley was smiling at the memory. He said, "You'd a thought everybody would've been down on Slade after that. But the girls in our class thought his move was smoother than silk. That's when Slade started getting friendly with the ladies. He saw that he had the power to charm women, and he's been working that charm ever since."

I nodded agreement. "Working it good," I said.

Foley said, "And now Slade's a major pretty boy who's got it all—the walk, the talk, the plan."

The sun had slipped behind a ribbon of clouds. Its

brilliance shone out from the cloud's tattered edges. I shifted my weight on the picnic bench.

"That's cool that Slade's been watching your back for all this time, Foley," I said, "but I'm scared. The Raven's got an evil mind of its own. I saw it in my bad dream."

Foley picked up the deck of cards and started shuffling them again, slow at first, then faster. His eyes met mine. He said, "Nell, Slade and me ain't gonna shoot nobody. The guns is just a way to get some running money. Don't make the whole thing more than it is."

Carefully, Foley began a game of solitaire. He set down a row of seven stacks of cards, one at a time, each stack ending with a card face up on the table. "That dream you had wasn't real," he said, concentrating on his game. "It was something your head made up while you were sleeping."

Foley flipped an ace of spades from the card deck onto the table. Then he flipped a king of hearts. Then another king, a king of diamonds. His face filled with a look of satisfaction. He was winning at his own game. "I'm the one with *real* dreams," he said. "The kind of dreams that *can* come true. Dreams of cutting outta here, like your old man did."

With the back of my hand, I wiped the tiny beads of sweat that were rising on my forehead. I said, "But my daddy left Modine to go to coll—"

"To college, I know," Foley interrupted. "Believe me, Nell, I've thought about college a million times. But I don't got it the way your daddy had it. He had all them good grades. People *paid* for him to go to college."

Foley looked off toward Earl's Impala. "My grades . . . well, let's just say that as hard as I try, you'd think my report card was some kind of custom stationery that belonged to a guy named Dean Franklin. That's because the whole paper is usually filled with Ds and Fs, except for in shop class, where I can always pull in a B-plus, and sometimes an A."

I straightened Foley's cards on the table. "As good as you are with wood, Foley, you deserve nothing but A-pluses," I said.

Foley shrugged. "That's nice of you, Nell. But hammering wood ain't never got nobody no scholarship to college. And even if it did, Mama probably wouldn't let me go. She don't ever want me to leave here, not after the way my old man split and the way your daddy stayed away once he got a taste of life outside of Modine."

I sat real still for a minute, just listening to Foley. He went on. "Mama, she just don't get it. Sissies hang with their mamas. That woman ain't ever gonna let me go away from her. She thinks she *owns* me. That's why I got to go, Nell. I got to know that I own myself."

I nodded agreement. Foley was right about Aunt Ursa. "But, Foley," I said, "what about Uncle Bingham—and Rawling? If you leave Modine, you'll be leaving them behind, too."

"Bingham's good for keeping Mama in check," Foley said. "And Rawling, he's cool. But they're also part of the reason I'm getting out of Modine. Sometimes, Nell, when I look at the two of them, all I can think is that I don't want to end up crusty like they are. Them two is like me and Slade were as kids— Shorty and Slim. But they're grown men, Nell. Grown men who ain't never been nowhere or done nothing."

Foley shook his head. "I know I can't never be a high-and-mighty lawyer like your daddy, so I gotta use what I can to make it in this world. And if the Ravens is it...well, then..." Foley glanced down at his winning hand of cards, then turned his gaze off toward the heat-blurred horizon.

Dad called again that evening. This time the line was clear, no static.

"Hey, honey."

"Hi, Daddy."

"What's cooking?"

"Not much."

"How's Ursa?"

"Fine."

"How's Brenda?" I asked.

Dad hesitated. "Brenda's Brenda."

"Oh."

Then Daddy asked, "How's Bingham?"

"He taught me to play horseshoes."

"No kidding." A tiny laugh came through the receiver.

"I beat him," I said.

"*You* beat *him*?"

"I scored ten points."

"You must've been playing by Bingham Grady's horseshoe rules." Daddy's chuckle grew to a full-out laugh. I started to giggle. "How do you know about Uncle Bingham's way of playing?"

"'Cause Bingham played by his made-up rules when he taught *me* to pitch shoes. I was twelve then, too."

"So you started with three points."

"From the get-go," Daddy said. "Did Bingham tell you how horseshoes came to be a game?" he asked.

"The whole story," I said.

Daddy made his voice scratchy and full, imitating Uncle Bingham. "These is the ugliest shoes my horse eyes have ever seen!"

"You do Uncle Bingham good," I said.

"And I suppose Bingham's done good by me. I could always count on him for a solid story. The one about the blacksmith and his talkedy horse used to be my favorite."

"Uncle Bingham's been telling me lots of stuff," I said. "He told me he has a reputation for horseshoes."

"That's right," Daddy said. "Bingham's known all over Wolverne County as a serious shoe man. Some folks call him Bingham Grady the Great," he bragged. "He takes a lot of pride in being called 'great.' And even more pride in being named Grady." Daddy spoke thoughtfully.

"Uncle Bingham also told me stuff about Pip's mama, Hallie, and how he taught you to drive his car, and how he made you leave Modine so you could go to college." I let out a careful breath. "And he told me about my mother," I said.

Daddy grew silent for a moment. A strange kind of quiet hung there between us. Then, in a soft voice, Daddy said, "Yeah, Bingham's good with memories, too."

"He misses you," I said.

With a slow, heavy sigh, Daddy said, "Yeah, I miss him, too."

10

On Friday, the day after Foley and I hung out in the yard, I went to Rawling's Fish Fry to pick up an order for Aunt Ursa. Rawling's doorstep smelled of stale tobacco and beer-fried porgies. Rawling stood behind the cash register, counting the afternoon's earnings. His face was turned down toward the money drawer. He didn't see me and Pip coming.

The sign in Rawling's door window hung between blue corduroy curtains. It said:

OPEN TUESDAY–SUNDAY
CLOSED MONDAY
LUNCH SERVED
11:30 A.M. TILL 3:00 P.M.
DINNER SERVED
5:00 P.M. TILL THE FOOD RUNS OUT
CLOSED FOR REFUELING 3:01 P.M. TILL 4:59 P.M.

Another sign hung below the hand-lettered cardboard:

FRIDAY SPECIAL
FRESH-FRIED PORGIES HALF-PRICE
DURING REFUELING HOURS
(3:01 P.M. TILL 4:59 P.M.)
FREE LEMON WITH EVERY FISH PURCHASE

It was 3:30. I gently tapped on the glass of Rawling's door. Pip clawed the straw threads on the welcome mat at my feet. "Rawling, it's me, Nell Grady. Me and Pip."

I leaned my forehead onto the glass. Rawling peered over the top of his glasses with his good eye, smiling when he saw me. He came to the door, unlatched its bolt-lock, and let me in.

"Well, if it isn't the pretty lady with the earrings." He looked down at Pip. "And the dog with an itch for scrounging," he said.

Pip moved past Rawling's ankles. He sniffed his way inside. The fried fish and radio jazz drew me in, too.

"Aunt Ursa sent me to pick up her Friday-special order. She'll have the usual."

"A pound of porgies. Cleaned, boned, and fried up—*without* the beer batter." Rawling counted out Aunt Ursa's requests on his stubby fingers.

Pip had found an ice cooler next to the bar and was lifting off its lid with his nose.

I slid onto a barstool next to the cash register so that I could talk to Rawling face-to-face.

First he looked at me, then down at Pip, whose head and front paws were into the cooler, lifting out an ice cube. "I thought picking up Ursa's fish order was Foley's job," Rawling said. "I've come to expect Foley every week—him and his red baseball cap that I can always spot coming down the street."

"Foley drove up to Sackett with Uncle Bingham to get some wood planks for fixing Aunt Ursa's picnic table," I explained. "Uncle Bingham can't lift the wood into his car by himself, so he took Foley to help. They won't be back till six o'clock tonight." I steadied myself on the barstool. "Aunt Ursa's making a pound cake and couldn't leave the house. She didn't want to miss the half-price special, so she sent me."

Rawling gave Pip a disapproving look. His glasses magnified both his eyes, the regular one and the one that wandered. "I'm glad Ursa sent you, but I can do without that putting-his-nose-where-it-don't-belong dog." A toothpick jutted from the corner of Rawling's mouth. Even when he spoke, it stayed put.

With his ice cube, Pip was playing a game of slide-and-chase on Rawling's polished wooden floor. "Hot as it is, I suppose Pip's entitled to a touch of something cold," Rawling said, leaning his elbow onto the bar. "I haven't seen a rainless August like this in ages. I wish the sky would oblige us with a drizzle, at the very least. Seems, though, that the sky's got her arms wrapped around the rain. She and her clouds are just holding on."

Rawling closed the cash register drawer. He put the counted dollar bills into a small metal box that he left resting on the bar. "How's Ursa?" he asked.

"She's fine."

"She cooking for the Commemoration?"

"Enough to feed everybody in Modine, Sackett, Denison, and all the other towns in Wolverne County," I said, nodding with each town's name to make my point.

"And your daddy, how's he?"

I sighed. "Good, I guess."

"He feed you porgies down there in New York?"

"Nope. We eat a lot of Chinese takeout, though—shrimps and scallops and crabmeat."

"Beer-batter fried?"

"*Stir*-fried. But my daddy's girlfriend, Brenda, she only eats steamed."

Rawling shook his head. "A waste," he said. "You need some real fish, child. It's a wonder you're not dead of starvation."

I shrugged. "Aunt Ursa says the same thing."

"Well, Modine don't got no take-outs that make *steamed* food. And goodness knows, I sure didn't get my belly by eating *stir*-frieds."

Rawling washed his hands at the sink behind the

bar, then dried them on the clean dish towel that was folded over the spigot. "I'll put on the porgies," he said. "You sit tight and watch that Pip don't lift the lid off my cashbox. I'll be in the kitchen frying, if you need me."

The lady's voice on the radio delivered a slow, easy song. I spun myself once around on the barstool. Pip settled down with his melting ice cube, licking and gnawing at its coolness. From the kitchen came the crackle of hot grease. And soon the sharp smell of sizzling fish filled the restaurant.

Rawling had turned off the air-conditioning—he only kept it on during "regular customer hours"—and the small room was getting hotter than ten Augusts rolled into one.

I opened the back door, hoping to get a drift of cool air. All I got, though, was more sunlight. So I waited outside by the train tracks, hoping to catch the breeze of a speeding locomotive.

There wasn't a train in sight, and I couldn't hear any wheel-grinding in the distance to indicate that one was coming. But when I looked down the tracks toward Modine Creek, I saw some kind of commotion. Beyond a telephone pole, where the train tracks ran through a clearing, two people were arguing.

I snuck down the tracks a little ways to get a closer look and saw they were two boys, two black boys. One of the boys was real big. Big as a man, almost.

He had large fleshy arms and a thick waist. A long chain of keys dangled from his belt. The other boy was smaller and darker skinned. The two were standing at the open trunk of a car, swearing awful curses. The trunk door blocked their faces. All I could see of the boys was their bodies, facing off. And I could see the car's license plate. It said DILL.

I stood real still and out of sight by the tree at the edge of Rawling's dirt parking lot. I didn't recognize the big boy's arms or chest or belly. But the smaller boy's shoulders had a familiar slope to them. And when I saw the black cap that boy was twisting in his hands, I knew it was Slade Montgomery. Even though Slade had developed muscles since last summer, he was no match for the burly kid.

The other boy hissed something at Slade, angry words that I couldn't fully hear, and shoved at Slade's chest. The thickset boy then slammed the car trunk shut. He got up in Slade's face and hollered, "Don't be messing with me in this heat! You still owe me for the Ravens! All's I want is my money."

Even though I was standing at a good distance, that boy's snarling voice rattled me from the inside out. Then he shoved Slade again, hard enough to make him fall. Slade's face slapped the dirt. He was coughing and spitting and shaking his head.

I hugged the tree. My breath grew short and heavy at the same time. I wanted to go to Slade, but there was no telling what that boy would have done to me.

That's when I heard Pip barking, and Rawling calling my name.

When Daddy phoned three days later, his voice rushed through the receiver. "Nell, honey, it's Dad. Put Ursa on. I want to thank her for the maple cake."

I glanced down the front hall toward the kitchen, where Aunt Ursa stood with her back to me. She was hunched at the sink, putting elbow grease to her sausage skillet.

"What maple cake?" I wanted to know.

"The one she sent me. It came in the mail this morning, wrapped up tight in one of Bingham's old shoe boxes. Not a bit of the cake was crumbled. And that cake was *good*." Daddy was talking fast and happy, like a child at Christmas.

"Did Brenda eat the cake, too?" I asked.

Daddy didn't answer. Then he said, "Brenda and I have decided to take a little vacation, Nell."

"Oh. To where?"

"A vacation from each other," Daddy said slowly.

"You split?" I fingered the tattered cover of the Wolverne County phone book, which rested on the front hall table. I could feel Daddy's upset coming through the phone line. "We're just taking some time off," he explained.

"At least you got the maple cake" was all I could think of to say.

"Got it just in time—in time to help me drop-kick my blues."

"Aunt Ursa knew about you and Brenda breaking up?"

"No, I haven't told her yet. But Ursa's got what I call a knowing soul. As much as I hate to admit it, she's always been able to understand what'll do me good before I understand it myself." Daddy let out a slow breath. "It was that way when I was growing up in her house, and it's been like that ever since, even from three hundred miles away," he said.

When I turned my eyes toward the kitchen again, Aunt Ursa was standing on the step stool by the sink, stacking clean dishes in the cupboard. Daddy said, "I'm gonna enjoy every thick, sticky slice of her cake."

"And when you do"—I tried to imitate Uncle Bingham the way Daddy had done before—"throw some milk down your gullet."

That made Daddy and me just laugh and laugh.

11

The following Sunday, I was in my bedroom changing out of my church clothes when I heard Slade's voice spring up from the yard.

"Yo, Fo! Mrs. G! Butterscotch! Is anybody home?"

I quickly snatched my church dress off its hanger, shimmied it down over my shoulders and waist, and buttoned it back up. "We're home, Slade! We're all just back from church!" I hollered toward the open window.

Aunt Ursa called out from the upstairs hall, "Simon—that you?"

"Who else it gonna be, begging for a souped-up mac 'n' cheese recipe on a Sunday afternoon?"

I stole a quick look at myself in the small mirror that hung from a wire over my dresser. My bangs hadn't lost their curl to the heat, but the skin on my face was shinier than Vaseline. *Sweat-dipped butterscotch*—ugh. I dabbed my forehead and cheeks with the T-shirt I was supposed to be putting on.

My poem danced in my thoughts:

So fine
Lips touching mine
All beauty is yours
Do you know you're divine?
Everything changed when I tasted your kiss....

I could hear the rhythm of Slade's smooth-talk, blending outside with the deliberate tone of Aunt Ursa's voice. It had been about two weeks since Slade had kissed me, and more than a week since I'd seen him with that other boy down by the train tracks. We hadn't spoken since that day in the cellar. Now, hearing Slade's voice sent me into a mix of love-buzz and worry.

When I got to the porch, Aunt Ursa was standing on the step. In one hand she held a new recipe card. In the other, two shiny tomatoes. As I struggled to open the stubborn screen door, Aunt Ursa was saying, "Good God, Simon, what happened to you?" I smoothed my dress under me and sat on the porch step.

Slade threw me a wink. "Hey, Butterscotch," he said.

"Hey, Slade." I crossed my legs.

"You wearing the dress I like." His eyes roamed from my bangs to my ankles.

"You look pretty dressed up yourself," I said, letting my eyes do the same.

Slade was wearing a silky necktie around the scoop collar of his T-shirt. The tie's knot rested just below his Adam's apple. Its striped fabric hung too long on him, long enough for him to tuck the necktie's pointed end beneath his belt buckle.

Slade went back to addressing Aunt Ursa, ignoring her question. "My moms told me I couldn't be coming over here looking raggedy, Mrs. G. She told me this was the Lord's day. That if I was coming to visit you on the Lord's day, I had to look presentable. So I dressed up for the Lord—and for you, Mrs. G. I wore me this fine-as-wine tie."

Slade *did* look fine. But Aunt Ursa wasn't blushing and carrying on as usual with him. Instead, she studied Slade with a concerned expression. "I'm sure the Lord is smiling down on you right now with all that silk around your neck, but what happened to your tooth, child?" she asked.

I hadn't noticed at first, but Slade's mouth was messed up. His pretty-boy smile had turned to the jagged grin of a jack-o'-lantern. A front tooth was chipped, and one of his bottom teeth was missing.

"That ain't nothin'," Slade said, leaning against the side of the house. He wasn't shy about showing off the gap where his tooth once stood. He poked his tongue through the crooked patch of black. "I been taking big bites outta life, is all. Deep, meaty bites—

close-to-the-bone bites. I'm a busy man, Mrs. G. You know how it is."

"Well," Aunt Ursa said, "I guess boys have been busy roughhousing since the beginning of time. Just be careful, Simon. Ever since you've been old enough to walk, Rochelle's been telling me how prone you are to skinning the black off your knees and elbows."

"Yeah, Mrs. G, I'm the pronest brother I know— skinnin', roughhousin', scrapin' off my black. That ain't good, is it, Mrs. G? You're right, a man's gotta be careful."

Slade had erased the worry from Aunt Ursa's face, but I couldn't take my eyes away from his broken smile. All I could think of was the awful fight I'd seen between Slade and that big boy who'd knocked Slade to the ground. I curled my lower lip under my own front teeth, knowing Slade had really taken a bite of dirt, that he was lying to Aunt Ursa. And there I was, committing another lie of omission.

Slade didn't pay his tooth any more attention. "Where's Foley?" he wanted to know.

Aunt Ursa tucked the recipe card in her waistband so she could hold the porch step railing. She eased herself down onto the step, where she sat next to me. The tomatoes rested in her lap. "For weeks I been waiting on Foley to shave down the doorjamb so the door won't stick. He's searching the cellar for a planing tool," she explained. "Don't worry, Simon. He knows you're here. I told him he could come out when he's found the plane."

Slade nodded. "Yeah, that door does need fixing. You know what's best, Mrs. G."

"Of course I do," Aunt Ursa agreed.

"And you probably cooked up my mama's mac 'n' cheese recipe, didn't you, Mrs. G?"

Aunt Ursa slid the card from her waistband. She smoothed its creases with the palm of her hand. With the card, she gestured to Slade. "When Rochelle was here helping me fill out the Commemoration permit, I told her she had too much cheese, too much condensed milk, not enough macaroni. That's why it was coming out soggy."

Slade folded his arms. He stroked his goatee with his fingers. He frowned and nodded slowly, as if he were concentrating on every last word Aunt Ursa spoke. "You sure know your way around mac 'n' cheese, Mrs. G."

Aunt Ursa went on, proud and sure. "What I forgot to tell your mama is to slice these tomatoes on top. They're from my patch over there. Tell her I said a little garnish goes a long way. I wrote it all down, right here on the card."

"Hey, thanks, Mrs. G. You know my mama can't cook for nothin', but she been right about one thing."

"What's that?" Aunt Ursa asked.

"She told me if I did good—wore a tie—on the Lord's day, I would be saved. And, yo, she wasn't kiddin'." Slade lifted the recipe card from Aunt Ursa's hand. "Mrs. G, you saved me from having to eat any more mushy mac 'n' cheese."

Slade had done it again. He'd softened Aunt Ursa. "There you go, Simon, charming the blue off this blue jay," she admitted.

"And the yellow off this butterscotch," I added boldly.

We all laughed.

But Slade was just getting started. He gently took one of Aunt Ursa's hands, and at the same time, clasped my hand, too. Something inside me sputtered. Aunt Ursa let herself giggle. Then Slade drew each of our hands to his beautiful lips.

First he placed a soft kiss on Aunt Ursa's calloused knuckles. After that, he pressed his fleshy lips to my bony fingers. Real smooth, he said, "Somethin' delicious for the lady who can cook. And somethin' even tastier for the babe who stirs me up."

Slade was leaning so close, I caught a sniff of his warm breath, which was sweet, like the day he'd first kissed me. Our eyes met... *So fine... Lips touching mine... All beauty is yours.... Do you know you're divine?...*

But when I glanced back at Slade's mouth, at his jagged teeth, there was something behind his *divine.*

I peered into his eyes a second time, deeper than before. Underneath all that homeboy suave, Slade's eyes looked scared.

I was tempted to tell Aunt Ursa right then and there about the fight I'd seen between Slade and the other kid, and about the Ravens.

But then Foley came into the yard, and I let the idea go.

Aunt Ursa asked Foley about the planing tool. "You find it?" she wanted to know. "I can't take another minute of that blasted door," she said.

Foley shrugged. "I looked all over down there, Mama, but I didn't see the thing. I'll keep an eye out for it. I know how much that door gets on your nerves."

Aunt Ursa twisted her lips to speak, but Foley spoke first. "Look, Mama, don't worry. I promised you I'd fix it, and I'll *fix* it."

Aunt Ursa shrugged then folded her arms.

Foley didn't say anything about Slade's messed-up mouth. Instead, he playfully clapped the bill of Slade's cap. "Hey, blood, where you get that happening necktie?"

"You like it?" Slade asked. "It's an Armani—designer clothes for the man who's going places."

Foley rested his shoulders and back against the house, next to Slade. "Hey, man, that tie looks good. Where can I get me one?"

Aunt Ursa's expression had turned hard. "Now, Foley," she scolded, "you got two perfectly good ties that Bingham passed down to you. They're hanging right upstairs in your closet."

Foley wouldn't look at Aunt Ursa. He kept his eyes on Slade. "Mama, please," he said. "Those ties are tired. How'm I gonna wear them anywhere? One's got horseshoes all over it; the other's got four-leaf clovers. Next you'll be telling me to wear Bingham's white shoes."

Slade said, "Fo, man, listen to what your moms is sayin'. A tie with four-leaf clovers could bring you luck, bro." Slade elbowed Foley. "Think it over, man. Meanwhile, you can borrow my tie." He loosened his Armani and proudly draped the silk strip around Foley's neck.

Foley's lips—and his puny goatee—curled into a little smile. Admiring the tie, he said, "For the man who's going places."

12

The next morning, storm clouds painted the sky mop-water gray. All day, we watched and waited and hoped for rain. Aunt Ursa kept saying, "Even a drizzle'll do."

But the sky stayed dry. Not a drop.

That night at supper, Aunt Ursa added an extra prayer to her dinner-table blessing. "Please, Lord," she asked, "send us a little drink of water for my tomato plants and trellis roses. And, Lord, if rain isn't in the plan, then give us the patience and strength to endure the heat."

"Amen," I said.

Foley shrugged agreement. "Yeah, this heat is a trip."

As Aunt Ursa began spooning up the kale, a knock sprang from the back porch door. Foley looked up briefly, then took a biscuit off the serving platter.

I followed Aunt Ursa to the door to see who'd come to visit. There, on the porch, stood a tall policeman. His head almost reached the overhead porch light. The badge on his shirt glistened under the light's pearly hue. He wore a serious frown.

"Evening, Mrs. Grady. Pardon me for interrupting your supper." Aunt Ursa's hand gripped the screen door handle. She kept the door closed between us and the policeman. Moths and mosquitoes clung to the flimsy door screen.

"What can I do for you, Lloyd? Everything's all right, I hope. You coming by about the permit for the County Commemoration? Bingham and I, we filled out the papers a week and a half ago. Sis Midley and Rochelle Montgomery were here helping." Aunt Ursa folded her arms. I drew closer to her side.

The policeman licked his lips before he spoke. "Mrs. Grady, there's been—"

"How's your mama doing, Lloyd?" Aunt Ursa rushed in before he could finish. It seemed as though she didn't want to hear what the policeman had to say. She sensed trouble. "I just saw her at the Traub Supermarket on Saturday, buying a heap of potatoes. She'll be making her red-skinned potato salad for the Commemoration, I hope."

"Yes, ma'am, her salad's the best, Mrs. Grady. But that's not why I'm—"

"I keep telling her to add some ham chunks to that salad. It'll give it the right amount of flavor. And when she mixes the potatoes—and the ham chunks—with the mayonnaise, she should stir in some of those dried chives they sell at over at Traub's." Aunt Ursa chattered on. She wouldn't let the policeman get in a single word. "Chives can turn the most bland...They got all kinds of spices now, too...Best thing is to boil the potatoes slow...Let them cool at room temperature...refrigerator dries out the..."

Finally, the policeman raised his voice over Aunt Ursa's.

"Mrs. Grady, I need to speak to your boy, Foley. Is he home?"

I glanced back at the dinner table, where Foley sat eating. He'd pulled his baseball cap low over his eyes. His shoulders were curled in around him. All I could see of his face was the tip of his nose and his goatee.

Aunt Ursa went on talking about the potato salad, as if she didn't even hear the policeman asking for Foley. "Your boy, Mrs. Grady. Is he home?" the policeman repeated, urgently this time.

Aunt Ursa let out a sigh. Quietly, she said, "He's eating supper right now, Lloyd."

But Foley had already come to the door. "What you want *me* for?"

The policeman looked down at him through the door screen. Foley lifted the bill of his cap, just enough to reveal his eyes. A scared expression formed on his face. I moved in close to Aunt Ursa and slipped my hand in hers.

"Has there been some kind of trouble, Lloyd?" Aunt Ursa's palm went cold.

"Yes, Mrs. Grady, there *has* been trouble." The policeman looked down at his shiny black shoes. He ran his fingers along the band of his police hat. After wiping the wetness that had formed above his lip, he said, "Simon Montgomery's dead, ma'am."

Aunt Ursa put her hand to her throat as if somebody had suddenly snatched the breath from her.

Foley stood there, his eyes fixed to his feet, his hands dug deep in his pockets.

My eyes raced from Aunt Ursa to Foley to the policeman. The skin behind my ears started to burn. "Slade's *dead*?" I had to make sure I was hearing correctly.

"Dwight Rawling found the boy shot near the train tracks behind his fish restaurant," the policeman explained.

"*Rawling,*" Aunt Ursa said softly, "is *he* all right?"

"He's fine, Mrs. Grady. My partner's at his place now, asking him a few questions. We're hoping Foley can help us find some answers, too."

But Foley had pulled his cap back down over his eyes. He backed away from us, shaking his head. Then, in a flash, he ran to the cellar and slammed the door behind him.

"I'm sorry, ma'am," the policeman said. "I'll only need a moment of the boy's time."

I was certain Aunt Ursa would go after Foley. But instead she said, "Leave him be, Lloyd. He'll talk when he's ready."

Now Aunt Ursa's arm rested gently around my shoulders. Tears had begun to trickle down my face. "How's Rochelle?" Aunt Ursa asked.

"Your brother Bingham is with her now. He was at Rawling's place when we went by to answer the call Rawling had made to the station to report the incident."

"How'd this happen, Lloyd?" Aunt Ursa hugged me to her. She offered me the soft comfort of her bosom. I buried my face and heaved with crying.

Lloyd was slow to answer Aunt Ursa's question. "We're not quite sure *how* this happened, Mrs. Grady. But down at the station, there's been talk of a gun ring that's come to Wolverne County. Somebody's selling guns to our kids. It's a wicked business that's made its way to Modine. Word has it that some of our own kids are the ones pushing the guns. That's why I want to talk to Foley, to see if he knows anything."

Aunt Ursa's body stiffened. "But, Lloyd, this is *Modine*. Those guns and shootings and evil business only goes on in the big cities."

"I'm afraid that's not true, Mrs. Grady. Simon Montgomery's the third teenage shooting in Wolverne County this year. We suspect it was another teen who killed him. And I'm sorry to say, his death may not be the last."

Aunt Ursa stood real still, forcing herself to listen. I could feel her trembling beside me. Silently, she began to weep.

"But, Lloyd," she said, her voice frail with tears, "I grew up in Modine. I've lived here all my life."

Lloyd nodded. "I grew up here, too, ma'am. This is my home. I've never gone away from Modine, except to serve in Vietnam. And now I got a war to fight right here."

The day me and Foley and Slade played down by the train tracks rolled into my memory. *So fine... All beauty is yours.... Everything changed when I tasted your kiss....*

My heart pumped a stunted beat. I burrowed my face even farther into Aunt Ursa's warm body.

For a moment, the three of us stood quiet. When I looked up, the policeman took a small backward step. He glanced at me, then turned his eyes to Aunt Ursa. "I need to go," he said softly. "But I'll have to speak to Foley, ma'am—when he's ready, of course."

Aunt Ursa answered with a single nod. As the policeman stepped off the porch, she and I stood frozen, like two brown statues clinging to each other. We watched Lloyd walk toward his patrol car. His body was a blue silhouette beneath the dusk sky. Before he pulled open his car door, he said quietly, "Look out for your boy, Mrs. Grady."

Aunt Ursa's arms had grown heavy around me. She didn't utter another word to Lloyd. But as she pulled me into the house, she softly repeated her protest, "I've lived in Modine all my life."

Aunt Ursa went straight to Slade's mother's house. "I'll be home soon, Nell. Stay back with Foley," she'd said. Then, over and over, she whispered "Poor Rochelle. Poor, sweet Rochelle."

I curled myself into a corner near the nook. With my knees pulled in close to my face, I lowered my head and wept. I was a jumble of uncertainty. Right then, there were only two things that I knew for sure: Our supper had grown cold on the table, and Foley wouldn't come out of the cellar.

13

From the next morning on, at every meal, Aunt Ursa put a tray of food by the cellar door. "You all right down there, Foley?" she'd call softly into the dimness.

"Thinking, Mama. I'm thinking, is all," Foley would answer back quietly. At each meal, the food on the tray grew cold. Foley would leave it outside the cellar, untouched. While cleaning up the wasted food, Aunt Ursa shook her head. When the next mealtime came, she'd put down a new tray.

This went on for two days. Two days of Aunt Ursa spending most of her free time with Rochelle, cooking for her, and helping with the arrangements for Slade's burial.

Uncle Bingham was busy driving Aunt Ursa back and forth between Rochelle's house, Traub Supermarket, and the Clifton Funeral Home, where Slade's body lay.

Most of that time, Pip and I were left at home, while everybody else was coming and going, and planning Slade's funeral. Nobody else came right out and spoke about Slade's dying. Once, though, I overheard Aunt Ursa tell Uncle Bingham that Slade had "passed on through the gates." That was the closest she came to acknowledging Slade's death.

After Slade was shot, my body took on the numb weight of Uncle Bingham's iron horseshoes. I slept off and on for two whole days. Each time I slept, a storm sky full of dreams swirled in my head, dreams that I couldn't fully remember upon waking. Most of them had to do with Slade and Foley and the Raven .25.

On the eve of Slade's funeral, Aunt Ursa made an early supper. I went straight to my room afterward, the chicken and squash in my belly threatening to come up. My mind couldn't make any sense of things.

Slade gone away... Slade shot... Slade dead.

With my body balled up on top of my comforter, I studied the picture of my mother for what seemed like the millionth time. But this was the first time I ever saw my mother's eyes looking back at me through my own face. There was something similar about the contour of our eyelids, the arc of our brows, and the upward swing of our lashes. "We've got the same grown-up lady eyes," I whispered, drawing the picture closer. We also had the same ample lips and prominent chin. The same slender neck and rounded forehead.

Soft and pretty, Lacy Nell Grady. That was my mama. And it was me, too. I wondered if Mama had "passed on" through the same "gates" as Slade, and if she would meet Slade in heaven.

I closed my eyes and saw Slade's pretty-boy smile. I remembered how it could turn me to maple syrup in an instant. Then I remembered one of the last times I'd seen Slade—behind Rawling's Fish Fry. He wasn't smiling then but grimacing with the pain of that boy smacking him to the dirt.

A warm breeze blew into the room, parting the curtains and slightly lifting the skirt on the flowered dress Aunt Ursa had washed and ironed and hung on the curtain rod for me to wear to Slade's funeral. It was the Sunday dress I'd worn on the day Slade had come visiting with his mama's mac-and-cheese recipe. Slade had liked that flowered dress. Slade had liked *me* in that dress.

Thinking about Slade yanked at my insides. I started to rock, then whimper. I gently lifted my mother's portrait off the night table. With my finger, I softly traced Mama's face along the strong curve of her cheekbone. Even though I took comfort in that picture, my belly turned loose a sob.

I hugged my mother's picture close to my chest. "Foley's got a gun, Mama, a Raven twenty-five, that he got from Slade—and *I'm* hiding it." I wiped my face with the back of my hand. "Slade had a Raven, too," I cried. "And now Slade's dead because of it."

I placed my mother's picture back on the night

table and turned off the light. I had disobeyed Aunt Ursa by allowing Pip to curl up next to me under the bedsheet. I clutched my pillow into my arms and held on tight, staring hard into the darkness, listening to the whispers and creaks of Aunt Ursa's pipes and roof shingles and floorboards settling in for the night.

Pip tried to lick my face clean of its tears. He snuggled next to me until I fell into a stone-still sleep.

Later that night, I woke with a start. The half-moon hung in a thicket of clouds in the black sky. Its light beamed into my room, across the edge of my comforter, and onto the corner of Dove Haven. The air was quiet, and dense with humidity.

I lay still for a moment, then slowly stepped onto the tattered rug by the bed, careful not to wake Pip, who was sleeping nearby on Foley's old coat. But Pip must have felt the silent weight of my feet on the floorboards. He lifted his drowsy head and looked me right in the face. "Shh...Pip—it's me, Nell." I knelt to give Pip's head and snout a stroke. Soon he was already back to sleep, letting out a little wheeze each time he breathed.

I went to Dove Haven to check on Foley's Raven—cold, black, heavy, trouble. The nasty thing, the "ticket" Foley was gonna use to leave Modine. I knew right then that I had to get rid of that gun. I was afraid Foley would be the next one found dead.

I carefully lifted the Dove Haven's roof plank,

praying the creak made by its hinges wouldn't rouse Pip. There it was, Foley's Raven .25. The moonlight put a pearly gleam on its handle. The rest of the gun gave off a cold black shimmer, even in the dark night.

I wiped my sweaty palms on the front of my nightgown. With both hands, I picked up the gun. It seemed heavier than before. And bigger than it was on the day Slade told me to hide it.

I held the gun close to my belly and begged my hands to stop trembling. But it was hard to keep steady. Fear rattled me from my bangs to the dirt underneath my toenails. With each step, I tried to keep as quiet as I could. I even held my breath so that I wouldn't make any extra noise.

Then, more startling than the night itself, I stepped on a cottony mound. Thinking it was the tip of Pip's outstretched paw, I leaped back. I reached down to find my socks. My dirty socks that Aunt Ursa had told me to leave by the washer in the cellar. With Foley down there mourning, I had been avoiding the cellar as best I could. I'd left my socks in a clump on the bedroom floor, near the night table. Now, here they were, spooking the living wits out of me.

I carefully switched the gun to one hand—my fingers still quivered—and crouched down to pick up one of the socks. Holding the sock's ankle between my thumb and forefinger, I shook it free of its wrinkles, then shoved the gun inside. I figured the sock would keep the Raven from slipping out of my moist hands.

I tiptoed past Aunt Ursa's bedroom (I could hear her gentle snores coming from behind the half-closed door), past the bathroom, down the stairs, through the kitchen, and onto the back porch.

The night was so hot, and more hushed than usual, except for the lonely call of an owl in the distance. On the porch, Uncle Bingham's rocking chair sat still. The moon lit the backyard tree. Its creamy hue beamed across the storm cellar doors, lighting Aunt Ursa's tomato plants.

Once in the yard, I glanced back at the house. For a moment, I watched Aunt Ursa's bedroom window, afraid I'd see a yellow lamplight come on in her room. But everybody was asleep, even the crickets, which tonight were not singing their usual chorus.

The grass felt long and prickly under my feet. Aunt Ursa would tell Foley to mow the lawn soon, I thought. And she'd tell him to make sure he mowed the weeds around Earl's Impala. The rickety car sat there, looking tired and stuck in its patch of dirt, like always.

My plan was to hide the gun in the glove compartment of Earl's Impala. I thought, *Just like in my old dollhouse, nobody'll ever look inside that musty car. I'll tell Foley his Raven got to be missing somehow. The gun will be safe. Pip won't find it again. I'll be free of my secret. And maybe, just maybe, Foley won't run off, if he doesn't have a gun to run off with.*

I went toward the car, real slow, the Raven .25 stretching my sock into an eerie shape. I poked my head into the window on the passenger's side of the front seat, then reached in to unlatch the glove compartment. I tried to turn its metal knob to open the compartment door. But the knob wouldn't budge. The panel was rusted shut.

I jiggled the knob, slowly at first, then harder and faster, using all the strength in my fingers. *"Open. Please, open,"* I whispered into the dark car.

But before I could coax the door free, an angry voice shot up from the backseat. *"What do you think you're doing?"*

I sucked in my breath and, at the same time, let out a yelp. Then I swallowed down the knot of air that was closing off my throat. "Nothing," I managed to say, "I'm not doing anything."

"You ain't never been good at lying, Nell. So don't even try it."

It was Foley, spread out, lying on his back across the sunken seat. From what little I could see by the light of the moon, it looked like he'd been crying.

14

Foley climbed from the back to the front, slid into the driver's seat, and leaned over to open the passenger door. He was still wearing the T-shirt and jeans he'd had on the night Lloyd came to tell us about Slade.

Slade's Armani tie hung around Foley's neck, held by a loose, sloppy knot. "Get in," he said.

My heart thrashed in my chest. "Foley, I was just...I was gonna...The gun, it was..."

"Put it on the dashboard." A loaded expression filled Foley's face. He gestured toward the gun with his chin. "What's that you got wrapped around my piece?"

"It's my sock, Foley. I put the gun in there because—" I reached out for the Raven as I started to explain.

"Leave it!" Foley hissed.

My hand jumped back faster than if I were putting it to a hot stove. "Don't touch that gun ever again," Foley ordered.

I tucked my palms between the underside of my thighs and the sticky car seat. "I won't, Foley," I promised. "I *swear* I won't."

"You wasting your time if you think the gun's gonna stay hid in the glove compartment. I already thought of that. I was gonna put the Raven there as soon as I got it from Slade. But the door on that thing ain't ever been able to open. This whole damn car's been broken for as long as it's been sitting here."

I was too upset to answer. All I could do was nod agreement and let Foley speak. His words came out in a steady stream as if he were talking to himself. "My daddy, Earl, promised he'd fix this messed-up car, but he left before he did. He cut out before I was born. I told Mama I'd have this heap of chrome towed, but she said no. She told me to leave it be. She said my daddy was coming back to pretty up his Impala."

"Maybe he is," I managed to say. "Maybe he is coming back, Foley."

"All my life Mama been saying Earl's coming home. And she talks about this car—*Earl's Impala*—like my daddy's still living here. Like he gonna come and take her for a ride." Foley yanked on the bill of his baseball cap, pulling the cap down farther over his eyes. "Earl—he ain't never coming back here. I know that straight as I know my name. Everybody in Modine knows it, too. But Mama, she keeps dreaming. Keeps on praying into thin air."

My eyes snapped between Foley's angry face and the gun resting on the dashboard.

"Far as I'm concerned," Foley went on, "I don't got no daddy. Never did, never will. Never."

"But you do, Foley," I said. "You *do* have a father. He's just not here right now, but he's living—somewhere." I slid my hands out from under my thighs. "Not like my mother, Lacy Nell. She *isn't* coming back. She *is* gone forever," I said softly. "Your daddy could be alive, Foley. You could still see his face someday. Someday soon, maybe. But my mother's face is frozen in a picture. Frozen like glass."

Foley licked his lips. "Yeah," he said quietly. "I seen your mama's picture. Folks is right when they say you two look alike."

We sat quiet for a moment. A low hum of crickets began to fill the air.

"They gave me my mama's middle name," I said proudly.

Foley shrugged. He briefly turned his eyes toward me. "I got my daddy's name for my first and middle names: Earl Foley. But for some reason, Mama only calls me the middle name. Not once has she called me Earl."

"Maybe it hurts her too much to call you by Earl's name," I suggested.

"I suppose," Foley said, "but people in town say I look just like my old man, same way as you look like your mama. People say I got a chin and nose like his. And when me and Uncle Bingham went to Sackett on that day to buy wood, the man at the lumberyard said he'd known my daddy. Said I got a walk like Earl's."

I wiped the perspiration on my neck. "Aunt Ursa said you got his wandering spirit, too. Got a need to get up and go."

"I got more than a need, Nell. It's like something inside me, pushing me out of Modine. And Mama, she makes it worse. It's like I said before, the woman won't let me tie my own shoes without pointing a finger—'Foley do *this*! Foley fix *that*!' " Foley winced with each expression of Aunt Ursa.

"She doesn't mean any harm, Foley. Uncle Bingham says she stays on you because she's scared you're gonna leave her, like Earl did. And like my daddy did. She figures the closer she keeps a watch on you, the closer you'll stay in her sight."

"Well, she got it backwards then. Her eagle eye makes me want to hide from her. Besides, there ain't nothing for me here, Nell. Modine's a dark pit that's getting deeper all the time. Dark and deep, like the grave where they gonna lay Slade's dead body." Foley was wearing a twisted expression.

Slade's dead body. Those words hung heavy in the night air. After a slow breath, I told Foley about the fight I'd seen between Slade and the boy with the car, and about Slade owing money for the Ravens.

Foley started messing with his Armani tie. He made its knot even looser. "You sure you heard right, Nell?" he asked. "Slade told me he got the Ravens fair and square." Foley looked at me straight. His eyes were tired.

I nodded. "I heard what that kid said to Slade. He wanted his money. That's how Slade's tooth got knocked out—the boy knocked Slade down. Told him to pay up."

Foley lowered his eyes. "Come to think of it, Slade never gave me a straight answer when I asked him about his teeth." He shrugged. "And it makes sense that Slade owed money. He didn't have any more money—or ways to earn money—than I got. But Slade would never admit to being down for the count. That was Slade's way, a pretty boy to the end." Foley shifted in his seat. He gave a heavy sigh, the kind of sigh that spills out after you hear bad news for the first time.

I told Foley some of what he'd missed since he'd been spending time alone in the cellar. "Tomorrow they're gonna bury Slade at Modine Memorial Cemetery, after his funeral at Aunt Ursa's church. I heard Uncle Bingham tell Aunt Ursa that the police said it looked like Slade was shot from close-up."

Foley squeezed his eyes shut. *"Man!"*

Neither of us spoke for a moment. Then Foley asked quietly, "They know who did it?"

"Nope."

Foley started speaking again as if he were talking to himself. As if he were talking his thoughts out loud. "Slade and me, we had a getaway plan. We wasn't gonna let Modine put its sorry hooks in us and keep us here to dry up with nothing to show for living. By the time we turned fifteen, we were gonna cut out of this place."

I listened, letting Foley go on.

"But Slade didn't even make it to his fifteenth birthday. This was the one time he couldn't sweet-talk his way clean. The gun that killed him was a lady he just couldn't charm. Now it's me that's gotta do the plan alone. And I don't see no reason to wait. New York. The big city of dreams. I'm gonna live the dreams Slade ain't never gonna see."

The crickets were singing fully now. "Foley, remember those soap animals you used to carve out for me?" I asked.

Foley nodded. "Last summer."

"And remember you said you wanted to be a carpenter?"

"Uh-huh."

"You still got a wish to be a carpenter, right?"

Foley shrugged. "Yeah. In fact, the man at the lumberyard in Sackett—the one who said I remind him of my daddy—he told me there might be some part-time work in September. Said I could bust wood and stock merchandise on Saturdays." Foley sucked his teeth. "But I can't sit around and wait for something that *might* happen. That would get in the way of me and Slade's plan. The man in Sackett couldn't make no promises. How do I know if there's really gonna be work like he said?"

"The only way you'll know is to stay in Modine, Foley," I said.

"I'd rather try my luck at getting some other kind of work in the city. Once I get there and sell my Raven, I can hook me up some connections, really make a go of it."

"Foley, you know what Aunt Ursa always says."

We said it at the same time—me like a statement, Foley like a question: "Good things come to those who wait."

Foley's hands gripped the steering wheel. The Raven .25, still wrapped in my sock, shone under the light of the moon on the dashboard in front of him.

"The stuff Mama says be in my head all the time."

"Maybe some of it you ought to listen to, Foley."

"I suppose." Foley pressed his forehead down onto his knuckles. He looked like a person who was praying.

"I miss Slade," I said, feeling wet come to my eyes. "And tomorrow we've gotta go to Mount Zion Baptist and tell him good-bye," I added.

Foley lifted his head. He fixed his eyes—they were

glistening with tears, too—on the moon, staring into its milky white face. "Uh-huh," he said. "Tomorrow's the day."

Foley lifted the gun off the dashboard. With his eyes still cast ahead, he tucked the Raven .25—sock and all—into the waistband of his jeans. "I'm taking it back. I need it now," he said.

I swallowed the thick saliva that rested on the back of my throat. My hands started trembling again. "But Foley—" I began.

"You done what I asked you, Nell. You kept my piece safe. Now go back inside and forget you ever saw the Raven. Get on to bed."

I didn't argue with Foley. I *couldn't*. I was too sleepy and sad and scared to speak another word.

When I glanced over at Foley a second time, at his face swaddled in moonlight, I noticed that Foley's goatee had grown to more than brush bristles. He had the beginnings of a real beard. The square arc of his jawline was tight with determination. And his eyes were filled with resolve, as if he'd come to some kind of grown-up decision.

As quiet as I could, I swung open the rickety car door and crept back into the house. The pale light of early dawn had begun to spread over the storm cellar doors, bringing with it the morning of Slade's funeral.

15

The smell of frying bacon woke me up. I stirred to the memory of summers past, when Foley would stick his head into my room and say, "Beat you to the pig strips!"

Now I lay on top of the rumpled comforter, my body heavy and tired from not getting enough sleep. The sun had already begun to scorch the day. I breathed in the blistering air. "More heat," I muttered.

Downstairs, a gospel hymn spilled from the small radio Aunt Ursa kept next to the toaster. I leaned off the side of the bed to peer through the floor vent.

The ironing board was set up in the kitchen. Foley's dress shirt, arms spread, lay across its length. Aunt Ursa was making breakfast and pressing the shirt at the same time. She worked between the stove and the ironing board, adjusting the flame beneath the cast-iron skillet and spraying starch onto the collar and cuffs of Foley's shirt. The steam from the iron, and the heat from the griddle, danced above Aunt Ursa's head.

On one of the gas burners, the flames licked Aunt Ursa's hot comb, which she was heating to curl my bangs. Aunt Ursa had owned that iron comb since she was a young lady. She refused to use a modern electric curling iron or a perm kit to smooth her hair. She called them "newfangled foolishness."

I dressed in front of the mirror. My hair needed taming, but Aunt Ursa would fix that.

I stepped back from the mirror to make sure my dress was neatly fastened, that I'd rubbed on enough lotion to soften my ashy elbows and knees, and that my slip wasn't dipping below my hemline.

Before I left the room, I lifted the roof plank off Dove Haven. The dollhouse attic, where the Raven once lived, stood empty. I huffed with a mix of relief and despair. I was free of Foley's gun, but now the gun was back in Foley's eager hands.

When I got to the kitchen, Aunt Ursa motioned to me with her spatula. "Sit down, child. Eat your bacon. I'll do your hair after you've had some breakfast." With one hand, Aunt Ursa shuffled eggs in the skillet; with the other, she turned down the radio.

Uncle Bingham sat at the head of the table, sipping black coffee. His dark suit jacket was draped over the back of his chair. He'd tucked a napkin into his shirt collar to keep himself clean. "Good morning, baby child," he said, offering me the chair next to his.

"This morning's not so good." I slid into my seat.

"I suppose I can't argue with that." Uncle Bingham lifted the tip of his napkin to wipe the shine off his forehead.

I set my bacon strips on top of my buttered toast, then folded over the bread to make a bacon-and-butter sandwich. It was my favorite breakfast, but I couldn't eat much of it. I just wasn't hungry. I snuck a piece of crust and a snippet of bacon to Pip, who had settled at my feet.

Aunt Ursa came to the table with the skillet in her hands. She served scrambled eggs to each plate. "Eat, Nell," she said. "You'll need your strength today." Then, with a sigh, she said, "I pray to God Foley comes out of that cellar."

I thought about suggesting that Aunt Ursa look for Foley in Earl's Impala, but I was afraid that would open up a worm-can of questions.

Uncle Bingham ate his eggs, while I picked at mine. Foley's breakfast steamed on his plate. With her fingers still bent around the skillet's handle, Aunt Ursa went to the cellar door. "Foley...," she called gently. "Come on up, son. We know this is a hard day for you. It's a hard day for all of us. But you need to eat, child. I scrambled your eggs with Dawson's cream, like you like them."

Uncle Bingham and I watched the cellar door as if its knob and hinges would somehow speak. Aunt Ursa continued, "I got your breakfast and your dress shirt all ready for you, Foley...Please, son, come join us at the table..."

But no answer came from the cellar. Uncle Bingham said, "Don't push him, Ursa. He'll come soon enough."

Aunt Ursa turned her eyes to the empty seat where Foley's breakfast was loosing its steam. "I'm worried about him, Bingham," she said.

"The boy's hurting, Ursa, but I don't think he'll want to miss the chance to bid Slade a restful passing on. If he isn't up here by nine o'clock, I'll go down and talk to him. You can't blame him for dragging his feet a little on a day like this."

"You're right, Bingham," Aunt Ursa agreed.

She set the empty skillet back on its burner and sat down with us to eat her breakfast. Her Bible, bound in ivory-colored leather, rested at her place setting. The radio music played on, filling the humid kitchen.

> *"Precious Lord, take my hand,*
> *Lead me on, help me stand."*

In a voice weighted with sorrow, Aunt Ursa joined the refrain:

> *"I am tired, I am weak, I am worn."*

Uncle Bingham pulled his napkin from his collar and wiped his face a second time. He sang along with Aunt Ursa, low at first, then in a full-out gospel harmony.

"Thru the storm, thru the night,
Lead me on to the light."

I closed my eyes and let their rhythm pull me up.

"Take my hand, precious Lord,
Lead me home."

Memories of Slade—Slade's bop, Slade's smile, Slade's kiss—weaved between the words of the hymn. When I opened my eyes to let my tears run, I saw a dark figure standing at the screen door. I couldn't see the man's face, though. It was cast in the shadow of the porch awning. "Morning, Mrs. Grady, I need a word with you." But once the man spoke, I knew his voice right off.

Aunt Ursa rose to open the door. When she pushed, it swung open freely. No more sticky doorjamb. "Lloyd, come in," she said.

It was the policeman—the one who'd told us about Slade's killing. Aunt Ursa was too caught up in her greeting to notice the door, but I noticed it right away. And when I thought back to the night before, I remembered how easily that door had swung open when I'd snuck out to the yard.

Lloyd was dressed in a black suit, not his uniform. Even though he wasn't wearing his police hat or badge, he stood just as tall, with the same steady stance.

When he stepped into the kitchen, his solid frame filled the tiny room. Pip lifted his head to give Lloyd a once-over. He barked two loud, feisty barks.

"Pip, hush now!" Aunt Ursa snapped. "Lloyd's a friend."

I fed Pip the rest of my bacon sandwich to keep him quiet.

"Sit down, Lloyd. Have some breakfast." Aunt Ursa inclined her head toward the table. But Lloyd wouldn't look Aunt Ursa in the eye. "No thanks, Mrs. Grady. I'm one of the pallbearers who'll be carrying Simon Montgomery's casket. They need me down at Mount Zion by nine fifteen. I can only stay a few minutes."

"I know you have to speak with Foley, Lloyd," Aunt Ursa said, "but this really isn't the day for that. Besides, he's not up yet."

Now Lloyd was peering straight down into Aunt Ursa's face. He gently placed his hand on her shoulder. That's when I noticed Lloyd's other hand nervously clutching Foley's baseball cap! He said, "Maybe you ought to sit down, Mrs. Grady."

Aunt Ursa must have seen the cap in Lloyd's hand,

too, because her posture suddenly turned rigid. She backed toward the breakfast table, groping for her chair.

Uncle Bingham stood up sharply. "What is it, Lloyd?"

Lloyd was slow to speak. The weather report— "unmercifully hot"—plunged from the radio. I brought my hand to the top button of my dress, the place where my chest muscles were starting to flinch.

Lloyd glanced toward Foley's empty seat at the table. The eggs on Foley's plate had turned orange. The bacon had gone from red to brown, and Foley's toast was now two soggy bread squares.

"I *am* here about your boy, ma'am," Lloyd said. "But I'm not here to speak with him... There's something else."

Aunt Ursa put her face in her hands.

Uncle Bingham slid his chair close to Aunt Ursa and sat down. He put both his arms around her shoulders.

I lifted Pip into my lap.

With careful words, Lloyd said, "Foley's run away."

Aunt Ursa shook her head. "No, Lloyd, you're mistaken. Foley's in the cellar." She was grimacing with denial.

"Foley!" she called out. "Foley, son! Come upstairs!"

Uncle Bingham closed his arms tighter around Aunt Ursa's hefty shoulders. *"Ursa."* He tried to calm her, but she was drifting into a state of unreasonableness.

Lloyd explained, "I worked the crack-of-dawn-patrol shift this morning, Mrs. Grady. When I drove down by the train tracks, I saw Foley jumping onto a freight car. I called out to him, but the train was barreling too loudly."

Aunt Ursa was still shaking her head. "Foley's in the cellar," she insisted. "He wouldn't run away—he wouldn't just leave here. *Foley!* Come out of the cellar." Aunt Ursa's voice rose to a shrill holler. *"Foley,* I'm calling you! *Foley,* can you hear me? Answer me when I call you, son. *Foley!"*

Then, as if somebody had snatched at her vocal cords, Aunt Ursa's tone dipped to a defeated squeak. "Oh, Foley."

Uncle Bingham held Aunt Ursa close. "Ursa," he soothed. "You're working yourself into a condition."

When my eyes met Uncle Bingham's, we exchanged a long, sad look.

Softly, Lloyd said, "Your boy's gone, ma'am, and I'm sorry to have to be the one to tell you—especially on this, of all days. But don't worry, I'll arrange a search team. We'll track down the train that came through Modine this morning. We'll find him, Mrs. Grady. We'll bring your son back to you."

Aunt Ursa was gasping softly as Uncle Bingham used his breast-pocket handkerchief to pat the perspiration from her face.

Lloyd slid two fingers along the sweat on his hairline. He gently placed Foley's crumpled cap on top of Aunt Ursa's Bible. "This was by the tracks," he said. "I saw it blow from Foley's head as the train raced away." Foley's monogrammed name partially covered the gold lettering on the Bible's jacket so that only one word stared up at us: HOLY.

Lloyd let himself out.

Uncle Bingham dipped his handkerchief into the pitcher of ice water that stood on the table with the breakfast food. He folded the cold compress onto Aunt Ursa's eyebrows and led her to the parlor. "Rest a moment, Ursa," he said, looking over his shoulder toward me and Pip.

I folded Pip in my arms. We pushed through the screen door and walked across the brittle grass to Earl's Impala. I slid into the driver's seat. Pip sat on the passenger side.

Just as I was about to lower my head to cry, Pip lifted his paws to reach for something that was resting on the dashboard. Gently, he pulled the item down with his teeth, placing it in my lap. It was my sock, and inside was a white bird carved from Ivory soap. A note had been fastened around the bird's neck. It hung from a string of fishing twine. My hands trembled as I read the inscription that was written on brown paper:

Dear Mama and Nell,

I had to fly.

Mama, I found the planing tool and fixed the screen door, like I promised.

Nell, the dove is yours.

I'll miss you, Butterscotch.

16

Aunt Ursa and I never made it to Slade's funeral. After she'd calmed down, she told Uncle Bingham, "You go on ahead. And take my condolences to Rochelle." Then, staring off toward the cellar door, she said, "They might as well be burying me today."

Before he left for Mount Zion Baptist, Uncle Bingham said softly, "Keep an eye on her, Nell."

I helped Aunt Ursa clear the breakfast dishes. We didn't say much as we worked. We were silent and thoughtful while the radio's gospel music played on. When the last plate had been washed and dried, Aunt Ursa lifted her Bible from the kitchen table and slid it under her arm, the same way she'd done so many Sunday mornings when we were heading off to church. With slow steps, she made her way to the front parlor, where she sought comfort in her reading chair.

"Sit with me, Nell, pray with me," she said, opening her Bible to the place where its ribbon marked the page. I sat cross-legged on the floor facing Aunt Ursa, my back resting on one arm of the sofa. I pulled a sofa pillow onto my lap, hugging it close. Aunt Ursa inclined her Bible toward the open window. As she read, her lips whispered a Scripture.

There were no words spoken between Aunt Ursa and me. We sat in that parlor for hours, silent. Each of us slipped into our own quiet thoughts, letting the morning turn to afternoon, then evening.

In the week that followed, Aunt Ursa stopped cooking. The crackling skillet sounds of hash and scrapple—and the sweet smells of dessert that usually came from her kitchen—were gone. We ate nothing but makeshift meals—cereal, mayonnaise sandwiches, canned mackerel.

Aunt Ursa was neglecting her tomato plants and trellis roses, too. The heat was beginning to wilt all of them.

Even Earl's Impala looked more decrepit each day. It was as though the car's tires had sunk deeper into the parched dirt. And the backyard clothesline took on a bleak sway without Foley's socks, T-shirts, and oversized boxer shorts adding their own special mix to the laundry.

Though the summer heat sweltered on, our house fell into a chilly silence. One night, as Aunt Ursa and I ate a supper of cheese on toast, I cautiously asked, "Are you *ever* gonna cook again?"

Aunt Ursa rested her elbows on the kitchen table. She pressed her fingers to the soft, crinkly hair at her temples. All she said was, "They've got to find my boy."

Each morning Aunt Ursa called the police station. "Any news?" she'd ask. "Anybody seen Foley?" she wanted to know. "All right, thank you, Lloyd." She'd sigh, then quietly place the telephone back on its hook, holding on to it for a long moment.

I kept trying to get her to call Daddy, but she wouldn't. I guess she was too proud to admit that she needed his help. I wasn't sure what I'd say to him, so I didn't call either.

The days crawled achingly slow, with no word about Foley. But Aunt Ursa's phone kept ringing, with people calling to send us their prayers.

Every time that phone rang, Aunt Ursa and I both jumped to answer it. Aside from Rawling and Uncle Bingham, Reverend DeKalb from Mount Zion Baptist called. And calls came from the people who worked with Aunt Ursa at Modine Creek Elementary. Rochelle and Sis called more than anybody—Rochelle in the morning, Sis at night.

Aunt Ursa kept every call brief. She didn't want to tie up the phone line, in case the police were trying to get through. After a while, she refused to answer the phone at all. Whenever it rang, she gestured at me:

pick up the line and don't talk long. When I'd tell her it was Sis or Rochelle, or anybody other than the police, she'd say, "Tell them I'm needing my silence, Nell, that I'm not up for talking."

The County Commemoration was two days away. And three days following it, I'd be on an Amtrak train, riding back to the city with a whole mess of strangers. Another August at Aunt Ursa's house would have come and gone.

Aunt Ursa hadn't said a word about the Commemoration. She hardly said anything about Foley running away, and she refused to talk about Slade dying. She wouldn't even discuss my going home. Most of the time, she just sat in the parlor, reading her Bible.

I wanted to tell Aunt Ursa about the gun Foley had with him when he left, but something had clamped down on Aunt Ursa's soul. Something was trying to steal her spirit. I was afraid that if I spoke on the Raven, I would snatch away the last bit of light Aunt Ursa had left. But still, by not telling her, I was back to committing another lie of omission.

I was stuck between what I'd heard Aunt Ursa call a rock and a hard place.

That night, I went to the parlor to check on her. Her body filled the stuffed chair by the window. She held her Bible open beneath the reading lamp that stood on the small table next to her chair. When I spoke Aunt Ursa's name, her eyes rose slowly off the page and peered over the bridge of her tiny reading glasses.

"Aunt Ursa, the Commemoration is the day after tomorrow," I reminded her. "All of Modine's waiting on your cooking."

Aunt Ursa stared at me blankly. "I don't have it in me to be cooking *or* commemorating," she said. "These days, Nell, I just don't have anything to give anybody." Her gaze slid back to her Bible.

I came closer to the arm of Aunt Ursa's chair. Gently, I protested, "But what about the money you were gonna raise for the marker to remember the black folks who first settled here?"

Aunt Ursa lowered her eyes back to her sacred book. "The desire's seeped out of me, Nell. It's gone from me. Things are different now," she said. "There's nothing for me to be celebrating."

With Aunt Ursa's face all tight and weary the way it was, I could see there was no use in trying to change her mind. I took a step back, out of the circle of light that surrounded Aunt Ursa and her chair. Standing in the lamplight's dim perimeter, I watched my aunt sink into another psalm.

Later, in my bedroom, I rifled through my panty drawer to find the train ticket Daddy had sent. His note spelled things out clearly, same as before: ... *give you a special privilege ... figured you'd like that. ...*

I buried the train ticket, deeper this time, underneath a mound of socks. "You figured me wrong, Daddy. Real wrong." I shoved the drawer closed with the heel of my hand.

That afternoon, another postcard had come from Tamilla:

Dear Nell,

Last night we ate at a place called Bella, one of the best restaurants in Venice. I stuffed myself silly. When the waiter came to clear our dishes, he said, "Where did that little girl put all her food, in her piedi?" Piedi means "feet" in Italian. My mother put baking soda paste on my mosquito bites, and the itch went away. Soon we'll be back at St. Margaret's—purtroppo! That means "ugh" in Italian! Non vedo l'ora di vederti. That means "I can't wait to see you."

Love,

Tamilla

P.S. How's Mr. Capital P?

I wrote back to Tamilla right then, so my letter would get to her before Labor Day, when she'd be coming home to New York.

Dear Tam,

I tried to make a meal for me and my aunt Ursa, but the only thing I know how to make is toast, microwave popcorn, and those cereal dessert snack things. Aunt Ursa doesn't even have a microwave. And for those cereal things, you need marshmallows. Aunt Ursa doesn't have those, either. So then I tried to make some scrambled eggs, with Dawson's cream, like I've seen Aunt Ursa do. But I burned the pan—and two of my fingers! And when I pulled my hand back away from the pan to suck at the burn, I knocked over the cream. Pip came quick to slosh it up. But then he tracked the cream-and-egg slop all through the kitchen. The whole thing was a big mess that I cleaned up myself.

I can't wait to see you, either, Tam. I have lots to tell you about Slade and a whole bunch of other things. It's stuff I can only tell you in person. Stuff I can't be putting in a letter to Italy. I'll tell you this much, though. I sure wish baking soda paste could fix what's wrong with me. My itching has turned to an all-out sting. How do you say "It hurts" in Italian? 'Cause it hurts bad.

Love,

Nell

As I tucked my letter to Tamilla into an envelope, I heard the phone ringing downstairs in the front hall.

I ran to answer it, not sure if Aunt Ursa would rise from her Bible reading. When I got to the staircase landing, Aunt Ursa had already picked up the call. I hung back quietly on the top stair, listening to see if it was news about Foley.

"*Wes!* Oh, Wes!" Aunt Ursa was crying. "I'm so glad to hear your voice..."

It was Daddy on the phone.

I wondered if I should close my ears to give Aunt Ursa some privacy. But I was too curious. I guess she really wanted to talk to Daddy after all.

Snatches of Aunt Ursa's words slipped up the stairs. When I heard her say "the Montgomery boy... Rochelle's child," I couldn't help but listen.

Aunt Ursa rushed to tell more. "Behind Rawling's place... A nasty happening... Too sad to speak on... A soul-sorry shame..."

Then, one final scrap of conversation floated to the landing. Before Aunt Ursa hung up the phone, I heard her tell Daddy, "Foley... missing... Train... Found his baseball cap... Never coming back..."

17

Late the next afternoon, Pip and I were watering Aunt Ursa's tomato plants, when we heard Buzzard, Uncle Bingham's old station wagon, clattering up Collier Street. Pip ran to the lawn's edge, yapping. And soon Buzzard's tires were crunching onto the driveway gravel.

Rawling was with Uncle Bingham, leaning his head out the front passenger window. "Hey there, Nell!" he called. "And how are you doing, Pip?" he asked.

I went to Uncle Bingham's side of the car and rested my elbow on Buzzard's door frame. "Where's Ursa?" Uncle Bingham wanted to know.

"Inside." I shrugged, catching a whiff of fried porgies spreading from somewhere in the back of the station wagon.

Rawling had gotten out of the car, and somehow Pip had leaped in. Together they were sliding a grease-stained carton and brown paper sack from the backseat. Pip's tail swished like kite ribbons in the breeze. With a smile rising in his eyes, Uncle Bingham said, "Nell, tell Ursa we're here."

I didn't ask any questions, but I sensed something good was on its way.

Aunt Ursa was asleep in her chair, her Bible resting open in her lap. She woke when I shook her gently. "Is everything all right, Nell?" she asked. By then, Uncle Bingham, Rawling, and Pip were in the parlor unwrapping a slew of packages. They'd brought fresh-fried porgies, a bag of lemons, a Tupperware bin of coleslaw, and a hefty loaf of squash bread.

"And here's a ham bone for Pip," Rawling was saying as he lowered the pink bone onto a plate he'd placed on the floor just outside the parlor doors.

As fast as I could, I unpacked the napkins and forks that were rolled up in a linen tablecloth from Rawling's restaurant. The cinnamon smell of Rawling's squash bread made my stomach sing with expectation.

"What on earth is all *this*?" Aunt Ursa was beside herself with surprise. She rubbed her eyes and sat up in her chair.

"It's some of the best food *on earth,*" Uncle Bingham said, spreading the tablecloth over the parlor coffee table.

"But who made—?"

"Ursa, you're not the only one who knows her way around the kitchen," Rawling said.

Aunt Ursa closed her Bible and set it on the end table next to her. "Well, nobody's ever—"

"And it's high time they did, sister. *High* time," Uncle Bingham said as he unpacked the last of the food and helped Rawling arrange it on the coffee table. They had even brought flowers. A mayonnaise jar brimming with daisies made a centerpiece for the feast that was spread before us.

Rawling placed a paper napkin onto Aunt Ursa's lap. Uncle Bingham went to the kitchen and returned with four tray tables. He unfolded one tray next to Aunt Ursa's chair, and set up three more around the parlor.

"Thanksgiving in August—and a surprise party, all rolled into one," I said.

"Sit back and relax, Ursa," Rawling said.

Aunt Ursa had grown fidgety with all the attention. "You can't expect me to just sit here and let you *serve* me." She looked from Rawling to me to Uncle Bingham.

Rawling said, "Ursa, try to think of this as supper at my restaurant, delivered to you at home."

"You don't deliver," Aunt Ursa protested.

Uncle Bingham pulled a lemon from the paper bag and quartered it with his pocketknife. "But Rawling's always taken pride in his service," he said. "Don't deny him that, sister."

I put my napkin in my lap. I was more than ready

to eat. The smell of the porgies had filled the parlor, and that squash bread was calling my name. Even the lemons looked good.

We all held hands while Uncle Bingham led us in a prayer. "Heavenly Father, these have been dark, uncertain days. But let us now feel the power of this circle of hands joined together—this circle that reminds us we are never alone, even in our blackest moments. We thank you, Father, for this food, and for the many ways you fulfill us."

Rawling gave a single nod. "Amen," he said softly.

"Amen," Aunt Ursa and I echoed.

Rawling served Aunt Ursa's plate first. "I haven't been too hungry lately. A sampling will do me fine," she said.

Rawling said, "Ursa, I've done up the porgies special, the way you like them. But eat as much or as little as you like. And remember," he repeated, "just relax yourself." He gave Aunt Ursa a small triangle of fish, a wedge of lemon, and a dab of coleslaw. He buttered her a thin slice of squash bread and carefully placed it on the edge of her plate.

The rest of us piled our plates with heaps of coleslaw and enough fish to fill Modine Creek.

I couldn't get my squash bread down any faster. It was still warm enough to melt the butter, and when its sweet crust slid to my stomach, I couldn't help but hum a sigh.

Aunt Ursa ate slowly and quietly, but she finished the food on her plate and asked Rawling for a second helping. "You got a recipe for this bread, Rawling?" she asked.

Rawling had cleaned his plate two times over. He reached into his breast pocket for one of his toothpicks. "I'm known down at the restaurant as the great improviser," he bragged. "I cook by the seat of my pants. Make it up as I go along. I got all my recipes stored up here in my noggin." Rawling touched his knuckles to his forehead.

"Think you could unlock your noggin and tell me the secret to making this bread? I'd sure like to know what's in it," Aunt Ursa insisted.

Rawling glanced over at Uncle Bingham. They exchanged a sly nod, as if they'd secretly won at something. Then Rawling leaned back in his chair and stretched out his legs, heels to the rug, in front of him. "I suppose I could put some of my improvisation to paper. But only for you, Ursa," he said. "Only for you."

"I'd like that, Rawling." Aunt Ursa reached for her third slice of squash bread.

Rawling took a clean napkin from the coffee table and a pen from his shirt pocket. He started to jot down his squash bread recipe on the napkin.

I swallowed the last of my meal, hoping someone

would ask Aunt Ursa about cooking for the Commemoration. But nobody mentioned it.

Instead, we talked about the "ludicrous" prices of lumber. We took bets on how high the pollen would rise once summer ended, and we poked fun at Pip, who sat by his plate guarding his ham bone.

Rawling tucked his squash bread recipe into Aunt Ursa's palm. Then he and Uncle Bingham slowly packed up the empty Tupperware, the loaf pan, and the porgy platter.

Forgetting herself, Aunt Ursa rose from her chair. "You leaving so soon?" she asked, neatly folding Rawling's recipe into her skirt pocket.

"I better be getting back to the shop," Rawling said.

"And I'm needing a nap. These past few days have been long ones," Uncle Bingham said.

Aunt Ursa took a deep breath, and with a large sweep of her arms, she hugged Rawling and Uncle Bingham at the same time. "You two" was all she said.

Uncle Bingham reached down and jiggled a daisy from the mayonnaise jar that he'd left on the coffee table. He curled Aunt Ursa's fingers around the flower's stem.

Aunt Ursa and I saw Uncle Bingham and Rawling to the door. When Uncle Bingham backed Buzzard out of the driveway, he called from the car window, "Nell,

Ursa, plug your ears! With this car, we don't have no choice but to leave as loud as we came."

Nodding, Aunt Ursa waved Uncle Bingham, Rawling, and Buzzard good-bye. Then Buzzard plodded away. The car's cranky motor grew faint in the distance.

We stood on the porch, watching dusk stretch its crimson cape across the sky. Pip had curled up on the porch step. He'd started to snooze. "Probably dreaming about that ham bone," Aunt Ursa said, resting her hands on my shoulders.

Soon, the sky was blacker than Aunt Ursa's bacon skillet. For a moment, the two of us looked out into the dark. Then, with a quick, tiny spark, a single star pierced the night.

18

Finally, and without hesitation, the sky opened its arms and turned loose the rain. The storm came late that night. It rained hard and noisy, with sheets of water that crackled like radio static. And, oh, the thunder—it boomed as if heaven's angels were having themselves a fierce bowling match.

But it wasn't the rain that sat me up in bed. It was the sweetness of what smelled like sunshine baking downstairs in the oven.

The kitchen's silken light streamed up into my bedroom through the floor vent. I carefully stepped over Pip and tiptoed downstairs. As I approached the kitchen, that sunshiny smell grew thicker.

Aunt Ursa was bent over at the oven, wearing her housedress. Her back blocked the oven's door. I couldn't see what she was fussing over, but its warm smell put me on a cloud. I stood in the kitchen doorway for a moment, watching.

With both hands, Aunt Ursa slid two pans from the oven. She placed them on the counter in front of her and tucked her pot holders in the pocket of her housedress.

The sky threw down another thundering boom. "Aunt Ursa," I said over the grumble, "you're *cooking*."

Aunt Ursa flinched and spun around. "Good Lord, child. You scared the gizzard meat out of me!"

I came closer to the counter where Aunt Ursa stood. I took a deep breath to make sure I wasn't dreaming. I repeated what I hoped was true. "You're cooking—in time for the Commemoration."

Aunt Ursa shrugged. "Rawling left his bag of lemons behind," she started to explain. "I was tossing upstairs in my bed, unable to sleep, pondering those lemons. I kept thinking what a shame it would be to let them go to waste. Then I heard the rain, and something nudged me to whip up two lemon-rind Bundt cakes." She waved toward the cakes with her pot holders.

Sure enough, two proud yellow mounds—their tops split open from baking—stood on a cooling rack next to the stove.

Aunt Ursa leaned on the counter, where she'd grated a small pile of lemon rinds. "Believe me, Nell," she said, "with all that's gone on, a picnic is the last place I want to be. As far as I can see, there isn't much to celebrate. But I figure we best get back to the business of living."

I went into the kitchen, greeted by the oven's warmth.

Aunt Ursa said, "The men and women who broke soil in this county lived through all kinds of hardship. But they carried on. Now that's what we gotta do—move through the pain. By attending tomorrow's festivities, we'll be honoring our elders, taking part in what they stood for—new beginnings."

I nodded.

Aunt Ursa said, "And since you and I can't finish off two whole cakes by ourselves, I figured the Commemoration's as good a place as any to take them."

"The Commemoration's the best place for those Bundt cakes," I agreed.

"I thought I'd do some meringue pies next," Aunt Ursa said. "Will you help me make the meringue, Nell?"

"Will I ever!"

I brought the egg carton from the refrigerator to the kitchen table. Aunt Ursa placed a mixing bowl next to the eggs and sat beside me. She showed me how to separate the egg yolks from the whites. "Now beat," she said, handing me a wire whisk.

I slowly turned the egg whites in the bowl. "No, no, Nell," Aunt Ursa instructed. "You've got to *whip* the whites—whip them till they're fluffy."

Aunt Ursa lifted the whisk from my hand. She hugged one arm around the mixing bowl and beat those egg whites good. "Like this," she said. The snap of her wrist jerked the whisk and egg-white batter into a liquidy blur. "Now you try," Aunt Ursa offered.

I cradled the ceramic bowl in the crook of my elbow and whisked as best I could. "Look at that, Nell," Aunt Ursa observed. "You've got a knack for making meringue."

"I do?"

"Most Gradys got some kind of calling. You may have found yours. Now keep whipping till you can't whip anymore. I'll take it from there."

My hand was already getting tired, but Aunt Ursa's words about my "calling" encouraged me not to give up so soon.

Aunt Ursa brought the rest of the lemons to the table. "These'll spike up the meringue," she said. With a small knife, she peeled more lemon skins off their fruit. The long, curly strips of yellow scented the room with a tangy smell.

"I missed your cooking," I said.

Aunt Ursa sighed. "It's a low-down feeling to miss something—or somebody—you love," she mused. "And it's worse when the missing hangs on to you."

Aunt Ursa took the lemon skins to the counter where the rest of the grated rinds sat. She washed her hands at the sink, then lifted a small black book from the dish-towel drawer. "My kitchen Bible," she explained, returning to sit with me at the table.

I had stopped whisking for a moment. As Aunt Ursa spoke, I rubbed the cramp from my wrist. "A *kitchen* Bible?" I asked. I'd never seen it before.

"I've got the Good Book stashed all over this house. The Bible's a boon in a moment of need. I have to have one handy whenever—and *wherever*—I can. For years I even kept a palm-sized Bible locked in the glove compartment of Earl's Impala. I'd forgotten about it until recently."

I started to beat the egg whites again.

Aunt Ursa continued, "I went to look for my tiny Bible last night after Bingham and Rawling came by with all that food. But the lock on the glove compartment was rusted shut. I couldn't open that confounded door to save my life. Then I coated the lock with a good douse of cooking spray and picked it with a meat skewer. When I finally coaxed the compartment door open, the book was gone."

After a brief silence, Aunt Ursa spoke with a little laugh. "Maybe a sparrow took my Scriptures."

"Maybe," I said, wondering if Earl had taken her Bible when he left Aunt Ursa and his Impala behind.

Aunt Ursa peeled back the jacket and pages of her kitchen Bible to reveal a vinyl pocket tucked inside the book's back cover. The pocket held a prayer card and a plastic bookmark, each bearing the face of Jesus.

One by one, Aunt Ursa slid the sacred items from the pocket. Beneath them, she'd hidden a muted

Polaroid, a picture of a man and woman perched on the front fender of a shiny car. The man's shoes had a gleam to them. So did the woman's smile.

As soon as Aunt Ursa set the picture on the kitchen table, I knew who that man and woman were. The man looked like Foley, but older. He had the same broad jawline and deep-set eyelids.

The woman had a strong nose and a soft swell of hair that framed her tiny face. There was no mistake about it. The woman in the photograph was a younger Aunt Ursa.

"That's *you*, isn't it?" I picked up the picture and looked at it close. "That's you and Earl," I said.

Aunt Ursa answered with a nod. Proudly, she said, "We're sitting pretty on the chassis of his Impala."

I couldn't take my eyes away from that picture. "Earl's got one of those full-grown goatees, like Foley's," I observed. "And he's got the same way of standing that Foley's got—one foot forward, like he's ready to take a step."

Aunt Ursa spoke with a hint of regret. "Earl and Foley are two apples from the same barrel," she said.

I tilted the Polaroid up a bit so that we could look at it together. "You sure were stylish back then, Aunt Ursa. That coat you're wearing in the picture is swinging."

"That's because it was called a *swing* coat. You see," Aunt Ursa lowered her voice, "when this picture was taken, I was three months along, expecting Foley. Nobody but Earl and I knew we had a baby coming, and I didn't want anybody to find me out. I had already raised one child born out of wedlock—raised him and watched him go off into the world—and that big coat was my only hope for covering up what was a family disgrace: me, the second Grady woman, unmarried and pregnant."

I gently touched Aunt Ursa's swing coat with the tip of my finger.

"I remember the day we posed for this picture. It was an autumn afternoon. Earl and I had just come back from a drive to Sackett, where we'd bought me the coat at Feldman's."

Aunt Ursa got a far-away stare in her eyes. "Bingham took this picture," she murmured. "Looking back, I think Bingham suspected that Earl and I had conceived a child," she said softly. "Bingham and I never spoke about it. But I guess it didn't really matter if we ever talked about it or not. After a while, everybody knew I was having a baby. My coat could only hide so much."

I took my fingers off the picture so that Aunt Ursa could draw the photo close to her face. I watched her lips quiver as she reflected on that long-ago time.

The storm had gone from a pounding rain to slippery smacks against the window. Aunt Ursa was wrapped up in her memory. "When Bingham pulled this Polaroid picture from his camera," she said, "he showed it to me and Earl, and told us we were destined to be together, just like Earl had inscribed in the tree out back."

"Earl and Ursa forever," I said gently.

"But," Aunt Ursa breathed, "the day after we smiled for Bingham's camera, Earl was gone."

A brief silence hung between us.

"Earl might still come back," I said quietly, realizing that I had believed that at one time, but that now I was just mouthing the same words I'd said to Foley on the night he and I sat in Earl's Impala.

"No, child." Aunt Ursa shook her head. "Earl's gone for good. And it's a false hope to think otherwise."

"But what about your faith, Aunt Ursa?" Now that I'd seen a picture of Earl, I didn't want him gone for good.

"I still got me plenty of faith, Nell," Aunt Ursa said.

The rain had stopped, but the thunder rolled on. Cautiously I asked, "You think Foley'll come home?"

Aunt Ursa didn't answer me right off. After a thoughtful moment, she said, "I don't know, Nell. I just don't know about Foley."

Then, smoothing the edges of her picture with her thumb and forefinger, Aunt Ursa made a sad confession. "What I *do* know, though, is that I held on to Foley too tightly. It was like clamping my hand around a bar of soap. The more I squeezed him, the more he slipped away."

Foley's Ivory bird fluttered through my thoughts. It was all I had left of him.

Aunt Ursa went on. "When I was in the parlor all that time after Foley ran off, I prayed and prayed that Foley would return to me. Then I changed my prayer. I started praying for Foley to be content, wherever he is."

I fingered the pages of Aunt Ursa's kitchen Bible. "Aunt Ursa," I asked, "is it bad to hope for things that could be unpleasant?"

"Like what?"

"Well, for the longest time, I wished that Daddy and Brenda would break up—and they *did*."

Aunt Ursa lifted the bowl of egg whites off the table and secured it in the crook of her arm. She picked up the whipping where I'd left off. I saw her trying to hold back a smile. "Nell," she said, "your wishing alone didn't bring that on. You see, you got *your* plan, and the Lord's got *His*. Sometimes they're the same plan; sometimes they're as different as night and day. But in the end, the Lord's plan is always the best for everybody concerned, even though it may not feel like it when the plan's unfolding."

I shrugged. "I guess this is a time when the Lord and I wanted the same thing," I said.

"Seems to be," said Aunt Ursa. She gave the egg whites a rest. Then she brought the Bundt cakes to the table, along with a box of powdered sugar and a tin sifter. "Let's top these cakes," she said. Dumping sugar in the sifter, she let me do the sprinkling.

As the velvety powder blanket fell to the cakes, I told Aunt Ursa the awful truth about Foley, a truth that I hoped she was ready to hear. I began slowly. "When Foley ran away, he had a gun with him. He said he was gonna hook up with somebody Slade knew, sell the gun, and try to get a job."

Aunt Ursa watched the sugar drift down from her sifter. She listened as I spoke. Her thoughtful expression looked as though she was opening herself to face what I needed to say.

I carefully and honestly told Aunt Ursa about getting Foley's gun from Slade and hiding it in Dove Haven. I told her how nightmares had plagued my sleep while the gun lived in my dollhouse, and how I tried to get rid of the Raven on the night before Foley fled.

The Bundt cakes were covered with white when my confession was through. I set down the sifter and folded my hands firmly in front of me.

Aunt Ursa's jaw tightened, but her eyes were kind.

She gently placed both her palms over my fists resting on the table. "Nell, that's an *awful* cross to bear." Aunt Ursa cast her eyes toward the strip of flypaper that dangled from the curtain rod over the sink. Shaking her head, she asked, "Why didn't you tell me?"

I licked my lips and turned my eyes away from Aunt Ursa's, staring off toward the cellar door. "I promised Foley and Slade that I'd keep it a secret. I wanted to tell you—I tried to tell you on that night in my bedroom when you were fussing over my dollhouse." I let out a short huff; it was as if I had to catch my breath. Then I brought my eyes back to Aunt Ursa. I looked at her straight. "I wanted to tell you, too, after Foley was gone, and you were spending all that time alone in the parlor. But I was afraid that if you knew about the Raven and Foley's plan, you'd be hurt real bad," I said.

Now our gazes wrapped around each other. "Sweet Nell." Aunt Ursa cupped her hands more firmly around mine. "I'm so sorry," she said. "You needed to speak your mind. But I couldn't listen. I *was* full of the fear of losing one more person I love, and so I closed off a dose of the love you needed from me. The love that it takes to hear the truth." Aunt Ursa sighed a breath of regret.

"You did the best you could," I said, letting my eyes find comfort in Aunt Ursa's generous expression.

"And you've listened to me *now*—that's the important thing."

Aunt Ursa nodded. "I hope to God that Foley's safe," she said, soft, like a whisper.

"I hope so, too," I said.

19

The morning was as golden as Aunt Ursa's cakes and pies. A ticklish breeze danced through my bedroom window. The heat wave's fever had been cooled by the rain.

Uncle Bingham came to drive us to Wolverne Field, the grounds where the first-ever County Commemoration was to take place. As we slid Aunt Ursa's pies and cakes onto the backseat, Lloyd pulled up in his patrol car. Pip sniffed Lloyd's shoes as he approached. Aunt Ursa's face filled with guarded expectation. "Have you found Foley?" she asked.

Lloyd shook his head. "Not yet, ma'am."

"What brings you then?" asked Uncle Bingham.

Lloyd hesitated before he spoke. "We caught up with a boy who says he knows how Simon Montgomery was killed."

I drew close to Aunt Ursa. Uncle Bingham stepped up behind me and gently rested his hand on my back.

"The boy's name is Dillard Chase, goes by the nickname Dill," Lloyd began. "You may know him.

He's a big boy—big hands, big gut, loud talking—drives a beat-up blue Buick."

My chest swelled with something heavy, something that was moving to my throat and pushing to get out. Even though I'd told Foley about the fight I'd seen between Slade and that boy with the car, I'd kept quiet about it to Aunt Ursa.

I stood real still, remembering the boy who had slapped Slade down. The license plate on his car had said DILL. He was the boy Lloyd was describing. That boy was stuck in my memory. Standing there, I knew that if I didn't tell about him now, he would haunt me for a long time coming. I took a slow breath, but no words came.

"Dillard Chase," Aunt Ursa murmured. "I know the Chase family. They live over in Sackett."

Uncle Bingham shrugged. "Years ago, I worked at Sackett Appliance with a Henry Chase. Dillard was his boy," he said. "Did he have something to do with Simon Montgomery's killing?" he asked quietly.

"Yes," Lloyd said. "He was involved but not fully of his choosing. As we'd thought down at the precinct, a small but powerful gun cartel is operating throughout Wolverne County. Dillard Chase was one of several gunrunners who got his pieces from a dealer, then sold them to other kids."

Aunt Ursa started to finger her gold-cross necklace. I could see her chest heaving slowly. My own chest was a knot of nerves. My heart slammed a stunted beat.

Lloyd continued. "Dillard had a whole mess of guns he was selling from his car trunk—MAC tens, Raven twenty-fives, forty-four magnum revolvers, and AK forty-sevens. He even had nine-millimeter guns, the same weapon we carry on the force."

I glanced down at the gun—the nine millimeter—in Lloyd's holster. The burden in my chest grew. Softly, I started to cry. Aunt Ursa drew me closer to her.

Lloyd went on with his story. "Dillard was earning a percentage on the guns he sold," he explained. "But most of the profits went to the head dealer—a trigger-man, they call him."

The sun was starting to spread its heat. Uncle Bingham pulled a handkerchief from his hip pocket and wiped the back of his neck. "Who is the head dealer, this triggerman?" he asked.

Lloyd adjusted his police cap. "Dillard's told us most of what he knows. We've got a name and some other identifying information, but we haven't tracked the guy down yet. You see, Dillard Chase was one of several boys caught up in a nasty web—a web whose sticky threads nabbed Simon Montgomery."

I was crying fully now; my breathing had become shallow.

"These crime webs can be very convoluted," Lloyd

said. "Dillard was only one small strand in the whole thing—a victim, really. After what happened with the Montgomery boy, I think the pressure got to be too much for him. When we took him into police custody, he ratted on the man he was dealing with. That'll lead us to some answers."

"What exactly *happened* with Simon?" Uncle Bingham asked, steadying his weight as if girding himself.

"The Chase boy told us that Simon owed him money for two guns—two Raven twenty-fives," Lloyd began. "Simon was slow to pay. Dillard said that he and the Montgomery boy were on fighting terms, always arguing about when Simon was gonna have the money. Dillard was getting heat from his dealer and putting that heat on Simon."

Aunt Ursa, who'd been listening very carefully, spoke up softly. "Simon was selling guns in this . . . this *cartel?*" she asked.

"As far as we know, Simon Montgomery was only a customer," Lloyd said.

With each word Lloyd spoke, I felt my throat pinch with dryness.

There was more to Lloyd's story.

"Two weeks ago—the last night of Simon's life— Simon went to the Chase boy and tried to work something out. Told him he'd try to somehow get the money he owed, but that he needed more time. But Dillard didn't have the time or the patience to wait.

The triggerman was on his case." Lloyd pressed his lips firmly together. He let out a weighty breath.

"So the boys started to argue, like they'd been doing for weeks," he continued. "Simon had a gun on him—one of the Ravens he owed money for—and the gun fell out of his jacket pocket while he and Dillard argued. Both boys scrambled to get the gun, and it went off. Simon Montgomery was killed by a wild bullet."

"God help us," Aunt Ursa whispered.

Now my breath was heaving in my belly.

"What is it, Nell?" Uncle Bingham asked gently.

Right then, it was as if the locked-up words inside me leaped out on their own. I was crying hard but managed to tell about the fight I'd seen between Slade and Dillard Chase. Then I told Uncle Bingham and Lloyd what I'd told Aunt Ursa the night before—that Foley had one of the Ravens with him when he ran away. Now I was speaking fast and urgent, my sentences tumbling on top of each other.

Uncle Bingham rubbed gentle circles in my back. "Easy, Nell, child. Tell it slow, now," he said.

"That Dillard boy was real mad at Slade," I blurted. "Real mad."

Uncle Bingham leaned into Lloyd. "You sure the killing happened like Dillard said—by accident?" he asked.

"We've been questioning him for a few days,"

Lloyd said. "And we've still got a lot of unanswered questions. Dillard's badly shaken, numb. But his story has been consistent. There are still a lot of details we're trying to sort out now."

My tears had stopped and the heaviness in my belly was gone, but my breathing was still unsteady. It was the shaky breath that comes after crying from deep down.

"We're still trying to get concrete answers about the gun cartel. With the description Dillard gave us, we've put the word out to precincts all over the state," Lloyd said.

Uncle Bingham nodded. He looked tired.

After a sigh, Lloyd said, "I'm not one for ruining a beautiful day like this, but I thought you'd want to know what we'd found out."

"Has anybody told Rochelle, Simon's mama?" Aunt Ursa asked.

"I've just come from Mrs. Montgomery's house," Lloyd said.

"How's she taking things?" Uncle Bingham asked.

"She was relieved to know the boy with all those guns is with police now. She didn't say much else." Lloyd lowered his eyes to the gravel that was under his shoes. "One of the worst parts of this whole crime," he went on as if he were mulling things over to himself, "is that we got brothers messing up brothers." He shook his head.

A thick silence hovered in the warm air. I took a deep breath and let it out slowly. Lloyd spoke into the stillness that had settled over us. "We're not giving up on our search for Foley," he assured Aunt Ursa. "We put a night patrol team down by the train tracks," he said.

Aunt Ursa took a small step toward Lloyd. "Thank you, Lloyd."

More quiet fell upon us. There was nothing left to speak on. Aunt Ursa inclined her head toward Uncle Bingham's car. "We best be getting on," she said.

Wolverne Field's dirt lot, where Uncle Bingham parked his car, was covered with night crawlers—some skinny, some coiled in the dirt, some shiny and wriggling, others oozing their innards from being stepped on or rolled over.

As people gathered, they cursed the ground with all its worms. But to me, those crawlers were welcome picnic guests. They reminded me of the laughs Foley and I had enjoyed together.

Wolverne Field lay just beyond the parking area. And oh, that field was a sight! All kinds of people had come to commemorate. There were lovers holding hands and stealing kisses, children playing tag and making threats with water balloons, and boys and girls getting smacked in the face with their own overblown bubble gum. Some people came to the field cuddling their babies. Others accompanied their elders.

Uncle Bingham cupped a hand over his brows to shade his eyes from the sun. "Look at all these people, here to enjoy a day of good-timing," he said. "They must've smelled your baking, Ursa."

Uncle Bingham's hand dropped from his forehead to his waist. "Folks have come out from the wood-work," he observed.

Aunt Ursa rested her arms across Uncle Bingham's shoulders. "Bingham," she said, "you can say you told me so."

While we unloaded the food and Uncle Bingham's iron horseshoes from the back of the station wagon, I watched people pass by on their way to the picnic tables. Some stopped to greet us, offering us kind words:

"So sorry to hear about Foley."

"May the Lord watch over you and yours."

"Wes's girl sure has grown."

Rawling came to the car carrying two folding chairs. "Good to see you, Ursa, Bingham," he said. He softly touched my cheek with the back of his hand. "Good to see you, too, Nell."

I shrugged. "Thanks."

Rawling rested his chairs against the side of the car. "I had to close up shop early last night, on account of the rain. Today, though—clear as can be. Perfect weather for a picnic." He glanced at Aunt Ursa's cakes and pies. "I know Bingham didn't cook up those desserts." He let go a little chuckle.

Uncle Bingham nudged Rawling. "As much as I'd like to take credit for those beauties, the praise goes to Ursa."

"It was the lemons you two left behind yesterday," Aunt Ursa said. "I just couldn't stand to waste them." She gestured toward me. "Nell had a hand in the baking."

I was sitting on Buzzard's fold-down hatch at the back of the car, letting my legs dangle. "I whipped the egg whites for the meringue pies," I said, snapping my wrist to show them how Aunt Ursa had taught me to do it.

"I guess the baker's touch runs in the Grady family," Rawling said.

"I topped the Bundt cakes with sugar, too," I bragged.

Rawling gave the cakes a second look. "You know anything about battering porgies?" he asked. "I could use another cook down at my place."

"Cakes and pies are my calling," I explained. For the first time in a week, Aunt Ursa laughed.

Rawling helped us carry our desserts to the tented pavilion that was set up for selling food. Then he brought his folding chairs, and he and Uncle Bingham went off to find the horseshoe pit.

"I'll save some dessert for both of you," Aunt Ursa promised, calling after them.

The food pavilion looked as though every cook in the county had taken to their kitchens. Beneath its canopy, a parade of tables showed off platters, plates, trays, and bowls of home recipes, done up to impress.

There were chilled butter beans, glazed hams, pickled beets, home-smoked sardines, deviled eggs, and pitchers of iced tea. And that was only for starters. People kept bringing on their goodies.

All that food made me blink. And Pip, he didn't know where to look first.

Aunt Ursa busied herself right away, helping the swarm of volunteers arrange the food to be sold. Sis Midley was one of the workers. She and Aunt Ursa shared a long hug as soon as they saw each other. "I've sure missed you, girl," Sis said softly.

"You been with me through all of this, Sis," Aunt Ursa said. "I could feel your support coming through the phone line—yours and Rochelle's."

Sis gave Aunt Ursa's hand a squeeze. "I asked Rochelle to come with me today, but like you, Rochelle's been needing her alone time," she explained. "It's gonna take her a while to start coming back around."

Aunt Ursa sighed quietly.

"But Rochelle used your recipe to make some mac 'n' cheese," Sis said. "I brought it here for her. Both batches are nearly gone already, and everybody's asking what Rochelle's secret is."

Aunt Ursa gave a humble shrug. Then she asked, "You hear about the Chase boy?"

Sis nodded. "A shame."

Aunt Ursa nodded her head in agreement.

The line of hungry people that had formed at the pavilion was beginning to snake out onto the field. "I best get back to work," Sis said. "People can get crotchety when the food stops flowing."

Aunt Ursa fixed me a plate. "Here, Nell," she said, "settle yourself."

But I couldn't eat. There wasn't a cake or glazed ham sweet enough to quiet the upset that still clung in my belly.

With Pip in the crook of one arm and my food balanced in the other, I settled under the leafy branches of a tree that stood opposite the food pavilion, away from all the picnic noise. I picked at the butter beans and deviled eggs Aunt Ursa had served me. Pip nosed at my food, though it seemed he didn't feel like eating, either. From where we sat, I could see the entire spread of the field. I watched the Commemoration carry on, with people swapping gossip, reminiscing, reuniting, and eating like tomorrow wasn't ever gonna come.

Apart from the crowd, I sunk into the comfort of solitude. Pip rolled to his back, feet dangling in the air, the same way he'd done on the day Foley had carved his likeness in Ivory soap.

Soon Aunt Ursa came over with a cup of lemonade and a plastic bowl of water for Pip. She was fanning herself with a paper plate. "Can you take some company?" she asked, standing back from the shade made by the tree. But the expression in her eyes showed me that she needed to take some time away from the picnic, too.

I nodded. "It's quiet here," I said. "The ground has dried from the rain, and it's nice and cool."

Aunt Ursa smoothed her skirt beneath her and carefully lowered her body onto the patch of grass next to me. "I can't say I'm in much of a party mood," she said.

"Me either." I shrugged, watching Pip slurp his water. "Uncle Bingham said the Commemoration would lift my spirits, but so far it's not working."

Aunt Ursa said, "It's gonna take a forklift from the Sackett Lumberyard to give my spirit a boost."

The food on my plate had gone limp. Pip started to settle for another nap, until an announcement sprang from the small speaker that hung from a pavilion rafter.

The voice, clear and loud, was Uncle Bingham's. "Starting in just five minutes, there'll be a horseshoe match at the pit on the west side of the field. This'll be a contest to end all contests! The first annual Commemoration shoe toss!"

Aunt Ursa raised her eyes toward the speaker. "He and Rawling have more than likely been practicing with those horseshoes since they left us at the parking lot," she said.

After a pause, one final shout bounced from the speaker. "Please come on over and put in a cheer for your favorite shoer!"

Pip shimmied beneath the speaker, barking at its noise.

Aunt Ursa got to her feet, and when I stood, I hooked my elbow around hers. "Uncle Bingham's calling us, Aunt Ursa," I said.

"That he is," she said. "Let's go."

20

As we walked toward the horseshoe pit, Pip followed along. Aunt Ursa said, "With all that Bingham and Rawling have done for me, I guess the least I can do is show them my support."

When we arrived at the pit, a small crowd had already gathered. They were waiting for the game to start. Uncle Bingham had his foot propped up on the iron stake that stood in the pit's middle. He was bent at the waist, wiping his favorite white shoes with a hanky. When he saw me and Aunt Ursa approach, he called us to him. "Nell, Ursa—over here. I need me some cheerleaders."

With Pip under one arm, I wriggled my way through the onlookers, who were hollering praises for their favorite players. There were four horseshoe throwers in all: Uncle Bingham; Rawling; Purdy Ford, a tall man with long arms and big feet; and Sis Midley.

"Purdy'll sew up the game before it even begins," somebody yelled.

Someone else hollered out, "I hope Rawling can pitch them shoes as good as he can fry them porgies."

"Show 'em what you're made of, Sis." Another shout popped up from the crowd.

I couldn't help but holler, too. "Stand by your reputation, Uncle Bingham!" I called through my cupped hands.

Even Aunt Ursa joined in. First she cheered for Sis. "Represent us women good, Sis." Then she cheered for Uncle Bingham, only louder. "Do the Gradys proud, brother!" she shouted.

Pip barked his own feisty exclamation.

Soon the match was under way. Sis pitched the first horseshoe. It hooked around the pole with a solid clang. "A ringer!" somebody yelled out.

Purdy Ford shot next. The open-ended U of his horseshoe straddled each side of the pole. "Purdy's pitch is saying something!" came the cheer.

Rawling's horseshoe landed almost on top of Purdy's shoe. "It's gonna be close," an excited voice called.

Uncle Bingham was last. His horseshoe smacked to the dirt with a muted thud. It was farthest from the pole. "More shoulder, Uncle Bingham!" I hollered. "Remember what you taught me about pitching— swing from your *shoulder*!"

Uncle Bingham looked over toward me and Aunt Ursa. He nodded, and sent us his two-fingered salute.

But as a follow-up to my rooting, somebody tossed out a jeer. "All the shoulder swinging in the world ain't gonna help a measly shoe toss like that."

"Don't you pay them any mind, Bingham. Just keep on," Aunt Ursa encouraged. Taking my hand, she worked to the front of the crowd. We now stood at the rim of the pit.

Rawling playfully clapped Uncle Bingham's shoulder. He spoke in a booming voice so everyone could hear. "You know what they say, Bingham, my friend. Your first pitch sets the tone for the whole match. I hope you got some kind of game plan, buddy, 'cause you've started off on the wrong foot. Even with my bum leg, I'm pitching better than you."

More folks had gathered. The crowd had grown to a thick mix of laughs, whoops, hollers, and praises.

"I'm just warming up, is all" was Uncle Bingham's out-loud defense.

But there was some truth to Rawling's words. The game unfolded as it had begun. And with each player's pitch, a new shout was flung from the crowd.

Sis's turn: "That lady sure can smoke them shoes!"

Purdy's turn: "Ford must have ate his garlic grits this morning!"

Rawling's turn: "Rawling *can* work them iron shoes as good as he can wiggle his skillet!"

Uncle Bingham's turn: "Bingham's got a lot of *boo-hoo*ing to do!"

Aunt Ursa and I kept hollering out praises, but nothing worked. Uncle Bingham went on losing. And to make matters worse, some folks—mostly people we didn't know—started to attack the Grady name. Somebody yelled, "As far as horseshoeing is concerned, it looks like the Grady glory is starting to fade."

"Yeah," somebody else agreed, "the Gradys will be *groveling* when this match is over."

Another voice chimed in, "Wolverne County will remember this as The Great Grady Disgrace."

The crowd's chiding was all meant in good humor, but Uncle Bingham's forehead was pinched with a frown.

Aunt Ursa shook her head. "Poor Bingham," she whispered. "His game is off today."

When Uncle Bingham's turn came up again, the taunts started in before he even had a chance to pick up his horseshoe.

But Aunt Ursa wasn't having it.

She marched to the center of the pit, where she raised her palm to calm the squawking. After a moment, the commotion simmered to a slow rumble.

Aunt Ursa spoke kindly, but her words were firm. She said, "Show my brother some respect, will you?" The onlookers gave Aunt Ursa their attention. "Bingham Grady has far from lost his touch. He just needs everyone to keep it down so he can concentrate on his game. The Gradys are horseshoe champs from way back," she went on. "Our legacy is alive and well."

For a moment, the swarm grew respectfully silent. Then, from somewhere deep in the fray, a single voice flew forward. "Speak on it, Ursa. We Gradys still got it!"

When I heard those proud family words, my heart grew to the size of an August watermelon. I knew that voice as well as I knew my own name.

Aunt Ursa turned abruptly to see who had spoken. Looking into the crowd, her hands rushed to her face. Soon she was gasping and pushing people aside.

Uncle Bingham rose up on the balls of his loafers to search the throng of people. His eyes grew happy with recognition. It was if he'd spotted an old friend.

Pip broke into a yap. I scooped him up to hold him close. "Daddy!" I called out. *"Daddy!"*

Daddy was sitting behind the wheel of his car, calling out his window. And there was somebody sitting next to him in the other front seat. At first I thought it was Brenda, but when I looked beyond the glare of the windshield, I could see that it was Foley!

Daddy and Foley got out of the car. Daddy was looking right at me and smiling the kind of smile you give somebody when you've just set a happy surprise down in their lap.

By the time Pip and I ran to where they were standing, Aunt Ursa had left a lipstick pucker over

Daddy's eyebrow and was squeezing Foley into one of her unforgettable hugs.

"Hey, Mama, Bingham." Foley greeted each one of them softly, a gladdened look filling his eyes. "Hey, Butterscotch," he said, nudging me, then smiling.

"Hey, Foley," I said.

Uncle Bingham slid his hanky from around his neck and started to wipe Aunt Ursa's kiss off Daddy's face.

"Now, Ursa," he said, "as much as I'd love to plant a juicy one on Wes myself, he can't be walking around with lips sitting up on his forehead."

With his hanky, Uncle Bingham gave Aunt Ursa a playful slap. "And, sister, give the boy some breathing room," he chided.

My heart was beating faster than Aunt Ursa's batter whisk. Pip had leaped from my hold and was dancing circles at Daddy's feet. "Hi there, boy," Daddy said, kneeling on the grass to let Pip lick his face.

"That dog will surely finish off the lipstick—probably thinks it's raspberry jelly," Uncle Bingham said, making us all laugh at once.

Pip started to lick Foley's sneakers.

"Pip, stop that," I warned.

Foley gave Pip's head a single stroke. "He's all right. Just actin' like a dog be actin', is all."

I crouched down next to Daddy. "You came to commemorate," I said, hugging his shoulders.

"And to pay tribute to the goodness of Modine," Daddy said. He looked up at Aunt Ursa and Uncle Bingham, and at Rawling and Sis, who had come over to join in the welcome. "I've been missing all of you," Daddy said.

Daddy stood up, nesting Pip in his arms. Uncle Bingham asked, "You still remember what I taught you about shoeing, Wes? I could use some pitching help right about now," he admitted.

"Swing from the shoulder, pendulum-style, right?" Daddy said, winking at me.

Daddy and the others walked on ahead toward the horseshoe pit, with Pip yapping behind them. Foley and I followed.

Foley had a settled look about him, like he'd found some kind of comfort. Without his baseball cap, I could see the expression in his eyes real clearly. The agitation had left his face; he looked satisfied. And the straggly hairs on his chin were all gone.

"What happened to your goatee?" I asked.

With his thumb, Foley traced the contour of his chin. "Your old man let me use his razor. He says the hair grows in faster once you shave it down."

Daddy, Aunt Ursa, and Uncle Bingham were up ahead, greeting people who were glad to see my father.

Foley and I had slowed our pace.

"What'd you do with the Raven?" I asked, sending a cautious glance.

Foley shrugged. "I hopped a train to New York," he began, telling me what I already knew.

I nodded. "Lloyd, the policeman who works the twilight shift down by Rawling's, saw you leaving," I explained. "He found your baseball cap by the tracks."

Foley reached for his head. He smoothed his palm over his hair.

"I did a lot of thinking on that train. A lot of hard thinking," he said. "I had all kinds of wild thoughts banging around in my head, enough to give a man a serious headache. When I got to New York City, I spent the night in the train station. Then for the next week, I went looking for Slade's connections. I was calling people, going to shady neighborhoods, trying to hook up with anybody who knew Slade. But none of the connections came through. The phone numbers were out of service; the addresses led me to dead ends. So every night, I went back to the train station, watched the trains come and go, and slept on a bench.

"My thinking was all crazy and muddled by then —and I was hungry for a real meal. The whole time, I thought about calling your dad, but I was too ashamed of how I'd run off—like his own mama and daddy had done to him. And then I got to thinking that by leaving Modine, I was doing the same fool thing *my* daddy, Earl, had done—turning my back, acting like a chicken-butt coward rather than a man.

Then, yesterday morning, I heard a voice clear as a train's whistle."

I listened carefully as Foley spoke. His words were so even, so sure.

"First I thought it was Mama's voice, talking in my head the way it always does," he said. "Then I realized it was nobody's voice but my own, telling me I was running in the wrong direction."

Foley and I stopped walking. We stood for a moment, just looking at each other, each of us enjoying the other's company.

Foley shook his head. "The more I thought about it, the more I knew good and well that my *connections* are right here, in Modine."

"Modine's got lots of good connections," I said, smiling.

Foley nodded. "That's when I called Wes, and he came and got me. It was real early when I called him. The sun had hardly cracked. I told Wes all about the Raven, and Slade, and the whole ugly mess, and he took me to the police so we could turn the gun over to them," Foley explained.

Right then, I felt something fall away in me. My insides got real quiet and calm. I think it was the thing Aunt Ursa calls peace of mind.

Foley went on talking, like he just had to get it all out. "I asked Wes not to call Mama right off, because of the shame I felt for skipping out on her. Wes agreed, but he told me Mama was sick with worry and that the only reason he wasn't gonna call her that minute was that he had an even better idea." Foley started to smile as he let his story unfold.

"We went back to your apartment in the city, where we washed up—that's when I used Wes's razor—and then we grabbed us some grub at this place called Doughnut Express. Next thing I know, Wes is talking about the Commemoration and I'm sitting in the front seat of his new car, on my way back home. And your pops has got that Christmas ornament I'd carved for him hanging from his rearview mirror. He's going on and on about it, and he's convincing me to hold out for that weekend job at the Sackett lumberyard in September. When we started seeing signs for Wolverne County, Wes says to me, 'You can tell Ursa to her face how bad you feel about leaving.' "

Now I was starting to smile.

Foley kept on. "And then Wes was saying all kinds of stuff about you, and Bingham, and Mama, and—" Foley hesitated. "And stuff about *your* mama, Nell," he said.

My throat was full of tears now. Good tears. The kind that don't quite make it to your eyes.

Back at the horseshoe pit, Daddy picked up where Uncle Bingham had left off. He pitched a good game, with all of us cheering him on every time his turn came up.

Sis Midley won the match. Daddy and Purdy Ford tied for second. Rawling graciously came in last place.

I wouldn't have cared a wink if each of Daddy's horseshoes had landed all the way over in Sackett. To my way of thinking, we Gradys had already won the summer's greatest victory.

ANDREA DAVIS PINKNEY is the *New York Times* best-selling author of several books for young readers, including the novel *Bird in a Box*, a Today Show Al Roker Book Club for Kids pick, and *Hand in Hand: Ten Black Men Who Changed America*, winner of the Coretta Scott King Author Award. Additional works include the Caldecott Honor and Coretta Scott King Honor book *Duke Ellington*, illustrated by her husband, Brian Pinkney; and *Let It Shine: Stories of Black Women Freedom Fighters*, a Coretta Scott King Honor book and winner of the Carter G. Woodson Award. Andrea Davis Pinkney lives in New York City.